MURDER IN SAN FRANCISCO

A Liz Lucas Cozy Mystery - Book 8

BY

DIANNE HARMAN

Published by: Dianne Harman
www.dianneharman.com

Interior, cover design and website by
Vivek Rajan

ISBN: 978-1979361132

CONTENTS

ACKNOWLEDGMENTS

Probably the most asked question I get from readers is, "How do you get the ideas for your books?" Here's the background on this one.

I have my husband, Tom, to thank for this book. He served twelve years in the California State Legislature, and prior to that, as an attorney specializing in probate law. While he was in the legislature, young men and women in our Armed Forces were being sent off to war in Iraq and Afghanistan. Many of them had concerns about having children in the event they were killed or badly wounded. To protect against such a worst-case scenario, some of them deposited genetic material with a sperm bank prior to departing for a combat zone.

Recent developments in the field of reproductive medicine have allowed human sperm and egg cells to be frozen and stored for many years, then by means of artificial insemination, successfully used to impregnate a woman.

As a former probate attorney, Tom became interested in what the inheritance rights were of a child who was conceived and born after the father's death. While he was in the legislature he authored a bill dealing with this subject, which was ultimately signed by the governor and became part of California law. His staff jokingly called it the "Dead Dads" bill. On the day the bill was up for a vote, one of his colleagues in the Assembly asked him if this was the bill about "Papa's in the freezer."

All joking aside, the bill provided needed guidelines and procedures for determining the inheritance rights of posthumously created heirs-at-law of a predeceased parent. In fact, several years after the bill became law, the U.S. Supreme Court, in a case arising in another state, referred to the California law with approval when it ruled that a child conceived after the death of his father was not eligible for Social Security survivor's benefits because the state in question had not adopted a law like California's.

Given the background described above, I thought it would be interesting to write a book about a dispute over inheritance rights when a child is conceived and born after the parent has died. Thanks, Tom, for giving me the idea along with all the technical legal advice that went into this book.

As always, my thanks to Vivek and Connie. You give my books the final touches that make them so readable and error-free!

And last, but definitely not least, to you, my readers, who make the long hours I spend writing so worthwhile. Thank you for buying, borrowing, and reviewing them. I truly appreciate it!

Win FREE Paperbacks every week!

Go to www.dianneharman.com/freepaperback.html and get your FREE copies of Dianne's books and favorite recipes immediately by signing up for her newsletter.

Once you've signed up for her newsletter you're eligible to win three paperbacks. One lucky winner is picked every week. Hurry before the offer ends!

CHAPTER ONE

It was a quiet afternoon in the San Francisco Police Department's Detective Division. Most of the other detectives were simply pushing some of their paperwork around, waiting for their shift to end, but not Mitch Latham, who was getting ready to retire in six months, and had something important weighing on his mind. He took one last look at the file in his hand, the file documenting the death of one Bernard Spitzer.

His chair creaked as he leaned back and reacquainted himself with the file one last time before deciding whether to put it in the large cardboard box labeled "cold case storage." Bernard "Bernie" Spitzer was eighty-three when he died. According to the coroner he died from natural causes, since no signs of injury or trauma were found on his body. Often the next of kin requested that an autopsy be performed, but in this case, given his age and the fact that there had been a number of homicides on the night the octogenarian died, his next of kin, as well as the law enforcement authorities, decided an autopsy was not necessary.

Something about Bernie's death made an alarm bell go off in the back of Mitch's mind, but he couldn't come up with any reason why. He doubted if Bernie had simply died from old age.

What bothered the detective was that Bernard Spitzer was a San Francisco legend, a multimillionaire, and whenever a man that wealthy died, red flags went up, but so far, he'd found nothing to justify them.

Instead, he had an octogenarian who had made a fortune as the founder of Spitzer Electronics, a company that twenty years ago had successfully fought off a hostile takeover by a corporate raider. Bernie had sold the company nine years ago to a Wall Street hedge fund for three hundred million dollars. He'd kept a minority interest in the company which paid him twenty million dollars a year.

The money alone could have been motive for a murder if he had, in fact, been murdered, but so far, there was not one shred of evidence pointing to his death being a homicide. Mitch kept reading, envious that a man of Bernie's age lived in the penthouse of one of the most expensive condominium projects in the city. After Bernie's death, Mitch had visited the penthouse and had personally seen the five thousand bottle wine collection Bernie had amassed over the years, which occupied all of the floor below the penthouse. It was equipped with automatic temperature controls to keep the various types of wine at just the right temperature. To a detective with the San Francisco Police Department, it was an unbelievable display of wealth, and put Mitch's wine rack containing a couple of bottles of sauvignon blanc and a Chateauneuf-de-Pape to shame.

According to the file, and from the conversations he had with Bernie's two adult children, Larry and Joni, Bernie had been widowed for the last twenty-five years and had enjoyed the company of a number of different women during that time. Evidently in recent years he had been seeing one woman exclusively, a woman named Michelle D'Amato. Larry and Joni didn't like her very much, but she seemed to take good care of their father, so they had grudgingly come to accept her, since they really had no choice. Neither one of them was particularly close to their father, and seemed happy to have any responsibility for him taken out of their hands.

"Mitch, time to give it up," his partner, Austin Grey, said as he returned to the small room they shared, a cup of coffee in each hand. He handed Mitch one of the cups, spilling it as he did so. "That Spitzer case was dead on arrival when it got here. Actually, it never was a case, just an old geezer who bit the dust. Trust me, from the conversation I had with the chief this morning, we've got plenty of other things on our plate that are a lot more important right now. Might as well kiss the case goodbye and send it off to cold case storage. Quite frankly, I think it's long overdue. I can't do the heavy lifting for both of us. Sorry to say it partner, but you haven't been exactly shouldering your half of the load for the last couple of months."

Mitch sighed, savoring the taste of the warm, sweet coffee. "Yeah, I know. It's just that since the guy died without a will and it's taking a long time to probate his estate, I just keep hoping something will show up that will justify these red flags I keep getting. Guess it isn't gonna happen. You're right," Mitch said as he picked up the file and walked over to the large cardboard box that held the dusty cold case file folders, dropping it in. "You're my witness. It's officially a cold case now." He smiled at Austin. "Sorry, buddy, I'm back."

"Good." Austin's face brightened. "I can use some help. Here's a couple of files that need our attention, like yesterday," he said as he handed them to Mitch. "Glad to have you back, partner."

FOUR MONTHS EARLIER
CHAPTER TWO

Four months earlier on a pleasant evening in San Francisco, Bernie Spitzer stepped under the striped awning and through the door of his favorite restaurant, The Seven Hills. The busy restaurant was buzzing with the chatter of people enjoying good food and company, and there was a line at the bar, but Bernie had no concerns about having to wait. He approached the maître d' who politely bowed and said, "Right this way, Mr. Spitzer. I've reserved your favorite table." He led Bernie and his female companion, Michelle D'Amato, to a table in the rear of the room. He handed them a menu and said, "Your waiter will be with you in a moment."

"Bernie, I know it's ridiculous, but I can't get beyond the ravioli when we come here. I'm hopelessly addicted to it." The auburn-haired beauty discarded her menu and reached across the table for Bernie's hand. Her green eyes met his through luscious lashes. Her pale, freckled skin was enhanced by only the lightest dusting of powder. Her rosebud pink lips were parted just short of a pout, revealing neat, white, even teeth and while several decades younger than her partner, she wasn't jail-bait, and she oozed a natural sophistication that caused more than one male head sitting at nearby tables to turn and look at her. "I wish I could make it like this."

Bernie squeezed her had. "Michelle, that's why I have the money. I can take you to places like this, so you don't have to cook. Let's face it, the Seven Hills Restaurant is the finest and one of the most expensive restaurants in San Francisco. That's one of the perks that comes with having founded, and then sold, a multimillion dollar business." He took a sip from his glass of the five-hundred-dollar bottle of wine that had been brought to their table as soon as they were seated and smiled at her. "This is quite good. I approve, but I probably won't tell them I have far better in my wine collection at home. I mean, what more could we want? A beautiful city, all the money we need, our health. Yes, life is good. Don't you agree?"

"Bernie, you know I totally agree, but it would even be better if I could have your baby. I know you've taken a vow to never get married again, and I understand and accept that, but if something happened to you, I wouldn't have anything of you. I'm not talking about money. I'm talking about you. I love you." Michelle tilted her head towards Bernie, causing her hair to curl up on her shoulder.

"Absolutely, emphatically no." Bernie said as he pulled his hand away from Michelle's. "The last thing I need is to have a kid. Made that mistake twice, and I'll never make it again. Both of mine turned out to be losers. Not trying a third time. Anyway, I'm too old to have a baby that needs to have its diapers changed every two hours and everything else that goes along with it. No, Michelle. Sorry, I love you too, but I am not having a baby and that's final."

Michelle's eyes flashed with hurt, and she decided to try a softer approach. "Bernie, the papers have always referred to you as the king of compromise. That's what happened when you sold your company. You got less than what you thought it was worth, and the buyers paid more than they wanted to pay. It was a good compromise. What about if we compromise?"

He looked at her suspiciously, even though he knew her background and understood why she was asking. The beautiful woman sitting across the table from him had been married three times, all of which had ended in divorce. She'd suffered two miscarriages, and was alone in the world. Her mother had left her on the steps of a church, and she'd spent her formative years bouncing from one foster family to another. When the last of her many foster fathers had recognized just how beautiful the young woman was and tried to sneak into her bedroom, she'd taken to the streets.

Bernie had met Michelle several years earlier when they ran into one another at prominent San Francisco law firm. She was there meeting with her attorney who had done a very good job getting a large divorce settlement from her wealthy banker husband. It hadn't hurt that Michelle had discovered he'd been having an affair with their maid. Bernie had been at the law office because his lawyer, Walter Highsmith, had insisted he come into his office and meet with him regarding his estate plan.

Bernie and Walter had spent the better part of two hours wrangling over who Bernie should leave his estate to and what should be done with it. At the end of the two hours, Bernie had thrown up his hands and said, "I don't care who gets it, because I'll be gone. When that happens, you do whatever is necessary. I'm done." He'd flung the conference room door open as he left the room and it narrowly missed hitting Michelle, who happened to be walking past the conference room at that moment. "Better luck next time," Michelle had said as she smiled and side-stepped out of the way. Bernie apologized profusely and asked if she'd join him for a cup of coffee. The fact that Michelle was so charming about him almost knocking her over had endeared her to him immediately. "I've been hit by a lot worse," she'd said as she tried to put him at ease.

One thing led to another, and strangely enough, within a few months the octogenarian and the beautiful young woman had fallen in love. They didn't bother to explain it to others, because they knew no one would understand how they could fall in love with that large of an age difference. Michelle simply loved Bernie, and he simply loved her.

He smiled, thinking of the happy times they'd enjoyed together since they had met, and his mood softened. "Michelle, I think you need to get away for a few days. One of the partners in the law firm I have on retainer lives in Red Cedar which is about an hour north of here. I've been told his wife has a spa there. Let me call Walter and see if he can get you in there for a few days. I think it would be good for you. My treat. How does that sound?"

Michelle paused before replying. "It sounds wonderful, Bernie." She leaned across the table and lowered her voice. "Look, I know you're trying to shift the focus away from becoming a father, but let me make one last attempt at this. I was at my doctor's this afternoon, one of those annual check-up things, and I mentioned to him that I wanted a child, and you didn't. My doctor told me a man could donate his sperm, and the woman could use it to get pregnant after he died. You said you didn't want a child while you were alive. Well, what about after you're dead? At least that way I'd have something from you." Her eyes widened, and she sat back again, folding her arms.

"Michelle, I'm sick and tired of this subject." Bernie slammed his menu down on the table and lifted his wine glass. "Fine, if that's what you want, fine. Give me the darned doctor's name, and I'll do it while you're at the spa. Will that make you happy?" he asked as he signaled to the waiter that they were ready to order.

"Ecstatic, Bernie, ecstatic." Michelle ran her tongue across her lips. "You'll never know how happy it makes me."

CHAPTER THREE

"Hi, sweetheart," Roger Langley said, as he walked through the front door of the Red Cedar Lodge and Spa. "What's for dinner tonight? Did the guests request anything special?"

His wife, Liz, looked up from where she was checking the visitors book at the desk in the spacious hallway. The space was filled with a soft glow from the setting sun outside. "We're having shrimp fettucine, mixed green salad, and something similar to bruschetta."

"Sounds interesting, what kind of something?" Roger asked as he walked over to Liz and kissed her on the cheek.

"Well, we have a garden in the back where Zack raises fresh vegetables and herbs for the dinners I serve the guests. I decided to use the garlic, tomatoes, basil, and a few other things that were growing in the garden, and I came up with something I think is wonderful. Trust me, you'll like it."

"Liz, I don't think you've ever served anything I haven't liked. Oh, by the way, I got a call from Walter Hightower today." Roger loosened his tie and set down his briefcase. "I don't know if you've ever met him. He's a law partner of mine who really brings in the big bucks for our firm. Anyway, one of his clients called and asked him if he could get a reservation for his lady friend here at the spa for three nights. I told him that would be fine and had him call Bertha. I told him we'd do a VIP thing for her and make sure she enjoyed her experience. I knew you wouldn't mind. Guess the client is some old geezer, but really bucks up."

"Sure. When's she coming to the spa?"

"She's already here. I saw her Jaguar in the parking lot with a personalized license plate that reads 'Bernie's'. I guess he got the car for her and wanted to make sure everyone knew both she and the car were the property of someone named Bernie."

"Sounds a bit like a male chauvinist to me," Liz said, closing the visitor book. "I mean, women are not the property of men."

Roger smiled. "Normally I'd agree with you, but this is a bit of a different case. The guy's an octogenarian and his lady friend is in her early 40's. Walter told me his client had no intention of marrying her, but he pays for everything she wants or needs. He even bought her a lush condominium two floors down from the penthouse suite where he lives. Walter said she's actually pretty nice and not the least bit of a gold-digger. I told him you'd make sure that her experience here at the spa was enjoyable, and as a personal favor to me, I'd appreciate it if you did."

"Of course, darling. Are you joining the other guests and me for dinner, or is this one of those nights where you need to prepare for court in the morning?"

Roger grimaced. "No court preparation, but I have a meeting with the partners tomorrow, and we're going to be looking at who gets a bonus this year, who gets an invitation to join us as a junior partner, and a bunch of things like that. I need to spend some time looking over what the courier brought me today. Hate to show up at the meeting and not have a clue what anyone is talking about."

"Okay, I'll hold the fort down. What's the name of Bernie's lady friend?"

"I believe Walter said it's Michelle D'Amato."

"When I go downstairs to change, I'll check my office computer, and make sure her cottage and the treatments she books are perfect. Don't worry, she'll get the VIP treatment. I'd hate to make you look bad in front of Walter."

"Trust me, Liz. You're not the only one," he said as he followed her down the stairs to their living quarters located on the lower level of the lodge.

*****

Later that evening, as the spa guests started to assemble in the lodge for dinner, Liz was greeting them and handing them name tags when the large room became silent as one of the most stunningly beautiful women Liz had ever seen walked in the front door. Her silky auburn hair was pulled back behind her ears that bore diamond earrings which Liz estimated to be at least two carats each. Piercing green eyes were framed with thick black lashes, which set off her porcelain skin and sculpted cheekbones. She had a smattering of faded freckles which were barely visible on either side of her nose. Her breathtaking beauty didn't stop at her face, but continued down the length of her voluptuous body, epitomizing everything both men and women coveted, although for different reasons. Despite her show-stopping entrance, the woman seemed oblivious to the sensation she'd created, and her manner was both friendly and unassuming.

She walked over to Liz and greeted her with a warm smile. "Hi, I'm Michelle D'Amato. You must be Liz Langley. I can't tell you how much I'm looking forward to this."

"Yes, I'm Liz and my husband, Roger, said he'd received a call from Walter, and that I should do everything I could to make your stay enjoyable. Please let me know if you need anything. The wine and cheese are over there on the sideboard. If you'll excuse me, I need to check on dinner," she said as she turned and walked towards the kitchen.

As Gina, the young woman who worked as Liz's dinner waitress and helper, began to serve the meal, Liz took the empty seat next to

Michelle and asked, "Have you had a chance to book your spa appointments for tomorrow?"

"Yes. I'm having a facial in the morning and a massage in the afternoon. I've also brought a couple of books with me. I noticed that there isn't a television in my cottage and quite frankly, I'm glad." Michelle giggled. "The gentleman I've been seeing for several years is hard of hearing and loves to have the television on, but unfortunately the sound is always turned up very, very loud. I'm looking forward to some peace and quiet."

"I can pretty much guarantee you'll get plenty of that here." Up close, Liz could see that Michelle was older than she first appeared, but whether she'd had any work done was hard to discern. Liz could only conclude that if Michelle had any botox or fillers in her face, they'd been done with an exceptionally light hand, which was rare.

"About the only sound at night is when one of my dogs, Brandy Boy, hears a guest in one of the cottages ring their bell, and he runs to the cottage to deliver a bit of the brandy contained in a small cask I have tied to his collar. He's been written up in several papers. Even if you don't like brandy, it's worth seeing, but a word of warning. He's so intent on getting to the cottage, he thinks anything in his way is simply something to be run over."

Michelle's mouth fell open. "You just jogged my memory. I remember reading an article about him in the San Francisco Chronicle a while ago, and I believe once, because of his rush to get to a cottage, he saved your life. Is that correct?"

Liz nodded. "Yes, it was several years ago, but he still thinks his reason to be on this planet is to deliver brandy at night. Trust me, the rest of the time he's pretty worthless. You'll see him lying on the porch and stepping over him is the only thing you can do, because he doesn't move for anyone."

*****

"Liz, dinner was wonderful," one of the guests said on the way out.

"I understand that a continental breakfast is served in the morning, is that correct?"

"It certainly is. The door will be unlocked, so please come in. We serve it from seven in the morning until nine. Enjoy the rest of your evening."

As they were leaving, every one of the guests talked about how wonderful the shrimp pasta with alfredo sauce had been, as well as the baguette garnished with tomatoes and drizzled with a garlic, olive oil and balsamic mixture. Several of them asked Liz if she'd be willing to share the recipes. Liz said she'd make copies of them, and they could pick them up at breakfast the following morning.

The last one to leave was Michelle. "Liz, thank you so much for a wonderful dinner. It was terrific, and I'm really looking forward to the peace and quiet of my cottage. It's so comfortable. You've thought of everything to make your guest's stay special."

"Good, I'm glad you like it. Is there anything I can do to make your stay more enjoyable?"

Michelle was quiet for a moment and then she laughed. "I feel like I'm committing a sin after that wonderful dinner, but I'm a sucker for a good hamburger. The gentleman I told you about thinks they're terribly plebian, and only for people who can't afford to eat at the best restaurants in San Francisco. I hope you won't be offended, but I think I'll go into town tomorrow and see if I can find a good burger."

"Tell you what." Liz liked Michelle's down-to-earth attitude, as well as thinking she could use a little extra weight on her. "I have to go into town and pick up a few things. There's a diner in town called Gertie's that makes a great hamburger, actually some say it's the best on the West Coast. People come all the way from San Francisco just to eat there. I know Gertie very well, and if you like hamburgers, you won't find a better one. Why don't you come with me? Believe me, meeting Gertie is an experience you shouldn't miss."

Michelle's face broke into a grin. "Who could resist a tantalizing proposition like that? I'd love to. What time are you planning on going to town?"

"I was thinking about noon. I can pick up what I need first, and then we could have lunch at Gertie's. What time is your facial?"

"It's at 9:30, so that should give me plenty of time. Shall I meet you here?"

"Yes, I'll see you then."

CHAPTER FOUR

Jim Brown's lip curled up as he threw the newspaper down on the ground at the park where he was sitting on a park bench and enjoying his cup of coffee. He hated the park with the screaming kids being wheeled around, dogs yipping because their owners were required to have them on a leash, and the homeless people who lived behind the hedge, shielded from the sight of the majority of the parkgoers.

He knew he was only separated from the people who permanently lived in the park by a very small margin, which was getting smaller and smaller with each passing day. The only reason he even bothered to come to the park was to read the morning newspaper that some San Francisco resident left there every lunchtime along with his empty five-dollar special made cup of Starbucks coffee.

In a previous lifetime, when Jim had been the co-owner of a successful company, Spitzer Electronics, he'd devoured the paper, anxious to find out what was happening around the globe, and more importantly, in the business world. Little did he know in those days that his partner in forming the start-up company, Bernie Spitzer, would find a way to take the company from him and then more or less throw him under the bus.

He didn't realize that he'd forgotten to file the patent for the scientific discovery he and Bernie had created. It was just that he'd gotten busy with other things. Then D-Day struck. He'd never forget the day that his world, no, his life, had imploded. He'd been working on a new patent when Bernie had walked into his office and with a triumphant chortle announced that he was now the proud owner of a patent, the very one for the product the two of them had invented.

Jim's chest tightened as he remembered how Bernie told him he'd suspected Jim hadn't filed the necessary paperwork to secure the patent, because he knew Jim didn't like to deal with details. Bernie had done a little digging and discovered that his instincts had been right, that their multi-million-dollar product was unpatented, and anyone could register it. Bernie told him that in the interests of the company and everyone who was employed by it, he'd filed the necessary paperwork, and since Jim hadn't bothered to do anything with it, he assumed Jim really wasn't interested in being a partner or even working for the company.

Jim's attempt at an explanation was not only unwelcome, but futile. Bernie had handed him a check for $100,000 which he said was Jim's severance pay. He'd had a security guard accompany Jim to his desk and watch as he cleaned it out, and then escort Jim out of the building. And that was the end of his career as the co-owner of a very successful start-up company.

The last twenty-five years had been a downward spiral for Jim. First his wife had left him, then in a desperate attempt to show her that he had a lot of money and she should reconcile with him, he'd lost the entire amount Bernie had given him in a Texas hold'em poker game. Losing the house they'd owned for years was the next disaster. He couldn't afford the monthly payments, and so the bank foreclosed. His social security income paid for the flea trap apartment he now lived in, but there sure wasn't much left over for things like newspapers.

And today, Bernie had once again, even after twenty-five years, managed to rub his nose in the loss of what should have been Jim's fortune. According to the article in the paper he'd just read, Bernie had announced that some of the money that rightfully should have been Jim's was going to go to some animal shelter. It wasn't fair, and Jim was at the end of his rope.

He knew it was too late for him. His life was over, but maybe in the twilight days or months of his life he could make Bernie Spitzer suffer as much as he had. It really wouldn't take much. After all, Jim knew a thing or two about science and drugs. Maybe it was fate that the woman next door to him was living with the night doorman at the condominium building where Bernie lived. He and the guy had even talked about Bernie once, although Jim didn't think he'd believed Jim when he'd told him he used to be Bernie's partner. Admittedly, he sure didn't look like some guy who Bernie would have anything to do with, but Jim imagined the doorman would probably let him into the building.

Jim pulled a sandwich wrapper from a nearby trash bin and pocketed the partly eaten remains, deciding that the newspaper article was a definite sign from the heavens above that he needed to do something before his time ran out. A plan began to form in his mind. It wouldn't help his financial situation, but it sure would help his mental outlook, and with his time on earth getting shorter and shorter with each passing day, it would be worth the risk to know that he'd finally taken action. Even Bernie could appreciate the irony about Jim not forgetting to do something. Maybe he'd forgotten to file the patent, but he'd make up for it with murder.

CHAPTER FIVE

Promptly at noon, there was a knock on the front door of the Red Cedar Lodge and just as Liz walked over to open it, Michelle walked through the door. Dressed in jeans and a flowing top, her makeup free skin was glowing.

"You're right on time," Liz said as her big boxer, Winston, stood next to her, quietly assessing the woman who had just entered the room. "This is my dog, Winston. My husband gave him to me shortly after we met. There was a bit of a murder mystery involving the spa, and Roger was concerned for my safety. Feel free to pet him, as he's quite friendly. He just looks scary."

Michelle bent down towards Winston. "You're not kidding. I'd never walk up to a dog that looked like him if the owner hadn't assured me the dog was harmless. He's a boxer, isn't he?" she asked as she extended her hand to let Winston sniff it.

"Yes, and he's absolutely the smartest dog I've ever been around. He was trained as a guard dog and is conversant not only in verbal commands, but in hand gestures as well, plus he's an absolute love. I can't imagine what I did before I had him. Let's go, my van's right outside," Liz said, as she opened the front door of the lodge.

Michelle followed her outside. "I can't imagine why you'd need a guard dog. Although your spa is a bit remote, I certainly don't associate your spa with a mystery."

"Unfortunately, somehow, I've found myself involved in several mysteries over the last couple of years, and all of them included murder." Liz unlocked the van, and they both climbed in. "Winston has not only saved my life on a couple of occasions, he's just wired to be permanently on guard. Hopefully, those days are behind me. To change the subject, how was your facial? And as the owner of the spa, I'm hoping you'll say it was terrific," she said with a laugh.

"Yes, it truly was amazing, and I'm saying that in all honesty. As a matter of fact, I'd say that even if you weren't the owner." Michelle reached up with both of her hands and smoothed her cheeks. "It really was the best one I've ever had. My facialist, Sonja, was very knowledgeable, and she even suggested a couple of things I could do to keep the inevitable lines on my face that are lying in wait from appearing someday."

Liz didn't mention her thoughts that Michelle might have already taken steps to prevent such an occurrence.

"My manager, Bertha, is in charge of hiring the spa employees and checking all their references," Liz said, as she drove the van down the lane and onto the nearby highway. "I remember her saying that Sonja received raves from her past employers. Since the lines of time have certainly made an appearance on my face, I think I need to make an appointment myself."

"Trust me, you won't regret it. I've had a lot of facials, and Sonja is now at the top of my list."

"Okay, you've convinced me." Liz said, smiling. They passed the rest of the short journey into town in a comfortable silence.

"I have to stop by the pet store and the market. You're welcome to come in with me or wait in the van. I won't be long at either one," Liz said as she pulled into a parking spot in front of a building with the name "Healthy Pets" on it.

"I'm here, so I might as well see what the people of Red Cedar are like. Liz, thanks again for letting me accompany you," Michelle said as she hopped out of the van and followed Liz into the store.

Forty-five minutes later, errands complete, they headed for Gertie's Diner. "I hope you're prepared to meet a real Red Cedar icon. I have no idea how old Gertie is, but whatever her age, I just hope I can be as active as she is when I reach it," Liz said as she pulled into a curbside parking spot half a block from the popular eatery. "Get ready, Michelle, because this may be the highlight of your stay in Red Cedar."

Liz opened the door of the diner and was immediately engulfed in a hug from a small slender woman who appeared to be in her 80's with back-combed bottle-blond hair and a pencil stuck behind one ear. She was furiously chomping on a big wad of bubble gum. After a moment the woman pushed Liz away from her and just stood looking at her.

Liz was the first to speak. Her face fell. "Gertie, is something wrong?"

"Course not. Jes' trying to see if you've changed during all this time you've stayed away. Staff was beginning to wonder if we'd had a set-to. Only thing that kept them believin' me was that handsome husband of yers' who keeps me in business and lets me know what's up with you, now that yer' so busy and all." Gertie stretched her face and clicked her false teeth back into place. "Been a coon's age, darlin', and that's way too long. So, who's this beauty you brung with ya'?"

Liz motioned towards her companion. "This is Michelle D'Amato, one of my guests. She mentioned she loved a good hamburger, and I told her you made the best one on the West Coast."

"Ya' got that right, darlin'," Gertie said as she turned and looked squarely at Michelle. "Gal, was you always that beautiful, or did the spa make you that way? If it's the spa, gonna have to pay it a visit. Could use a little gasoline in my tank for the new guy I'm seein'," she said with a leering wink. "Got me some new unders, but probably wouldn't hurt to do a little somethin' fer the chassis."

Michelle was clearly at a loss for words, her eyes as wide as saucers, so Liz answered for her. "In answer to your question, Gertie, yes, she was this beautiful before she came to the spa, but if you want to come, I'd love it if you'd visit as my guest."

"If'n ya' can't take thirty or some years off this chassis, think I'll give it a pass, but I'll keep it in mind if an emergency comes up. Got a nice little table fer you two at the back." They followed Gertie across the room to a table in the far corner of the diner. "Ya' can see who all's here, but the rest of the eaters don't usually look that far back." Gertie took the pencil from behind her ear and started to write, "So, Liz, two orders of your usual? A hamburger with everything and a chocolate malted milkshake?"

Liz looked over at Michelle who nodded affirmatively.

Gertie blew a giant pink bubble that splattered seconds later on her face. Peeling it off, she stuffed the gum back in her mouth. "Be back in a few minutes. You gals enjoy yerselves'. Liz, I not only missed you, I missed that big brute of a dog of yers'. Don't come back unless ya' got Winston with ya'. Hear?" With that, she hightailed it off to the kitchen to place their orders.

Michelle's gaze followed the elderly dynamo who tottered away on impossibly high heels. There was a running weekly bet among the diner's regulars as to when Gertie would take a tumble and have to do away with the stilettos. So far no one had collected on it.

CHAPTER SIX

Larry Spitzer threw down the business section of the newspaper he was reading and softly swore under his breath. There was nothing that irritated him more than reading that his father, Bernie Spitzer, had once again donated a large amount of money to some charity and given him nothing.

Stupid dogs, he thought. *If no one ever adopts them, so what. Might as well get rid of them, but no, the big man decided to give the shelter a boatload of money, so it could become a no-kill shelter. Like we need a few more dogs in the world. Why can't he ever give me a check that big? After all, as his son, I'm more deserving than those stupid dogs.*

He knew his luck was running out. The last get-rich-quick scheme he'd been involved in had cost him nearly everything he had, and there were no prospects for pot of gold rainbows in his future.

In a rare moment of introspection, Larry rested his head in his hands and looked back over the past few years and couldn't even begin to count up the number of things he'd been involved in that always promised, to his way of thinking, to make him a rich man, maybe as rich as his father.

It wasn't his fault that he really didn't have a profession to fall back on. That stupid teacher in college was the one who'd ruined any future career he might have had working in what people often referred to as respectable professions. He grimaced at the memory. When she found the answers to the exam Larry and the other students were taking stuffed up Larry's sleeve, it hadn't helped when she'd also found his stash of cocaine. The police were called and that was Larry's first arrest.

Over the years there had been other arrests as well as stints in several drug rehabilitation centers. As he played back the events of the last few years, one ran into another. Even though his father had always bailed him out, Larry knew how disappointed Bernie was in his son. Larry wondered to himself why Bernie had never understood that it really wasn't Larry's fault. It was all that professor's. He was sure he'd been targeted by the teacher just because he was Bernie's son.

When his mother had been alive, she'd always taken Larry's side and using reason, had logically explained to Bernie why Larry really wasn't to blame for whatever the problem of the month was. When she died, Larry's major cheerleader had also died. Since that time, Bernie had grudgingly helped his son, but the help had a hefty price tag attached to it. It had varied over the years, but the latest price tag was the threat that if Larry didn't clean up his act, become gainfully employed, and indicate he was free from drug use, Bernie was going to disinherit him.

Larry hated to admit it, but for years he'd been desperately counting on his inheritance. Truth be told, he'd been counting on it for as long as he could remember. What he hadn't counted on was Bernie living until he was over eighty years of age and still going strong. Larry knew it wasn't politically correct to wish that your father would die, but that was the only thing that could end the harassing calls from the debt collectors that he was now receiving 24/7.

He used to think every time the phone rang it was someone calling to tell him he'd won the lottery or one of his "investments" had paid off. Not anymore. He'd even started hiding his car in a friend's garage, because he was sure if it was parked on the street near the run-down apartment building where he lived, it would be repossessed. It really wasn't his fault life had dealt him a bad hand. He knew from the comments that people made that they envied him being the son of one of the wealthiest men in San Francisco. They didn't know that if his father disinherited him, it wouldn't matter what their relationship was. No money was simply that, no money, and from what his sister had told him, he wasn't the only one who had been threatened with disinheritance.

Although Larry had an arrest record, and there had been a lot of drug activity in his life, he'd always prided himself on the fact that he'd never had to resort to violence. Well, other than the one time when his second wife, Gloria, had gotten really mouthy, and he'd meant to merely tap her on the chin to get her attention. He still wasn't real sure what had happened, because the rage that had overcome him had clouded his memory, but the next thing he knew he was in police custody and charged with domestic violence.

When he'd returned to their squalid little apartment, Gloria was gone, along with anything of value, which wasn't much. The only thing she'd left was a note telling him that she'd put up with his dysfunction long enough, whatever that meant. He hadn't been too surprised, because you'd have to be a fool not to realize the marriage had been over for a long time. And Larry knew he wasn't a fool, just very unlucky.

The more he thought about it, the clearer it became to him that he needed to take control of his own destiny, and if that fate included something happening to his father, well, so be it. Like the expiration date on some of his prescription drugs his doctor had prescribed, he figured Bernie had outlived his expiration date, particularly if that date involved disinheritance.

CHAPTER SEVEN

As she sat looking out the front window of her modest home onto the littered front yards of the neighbors, Joni Toscano relived the conversation she'd had a few days earlier with her father, Bernie Spitzer. Her husband, Rocco, would be home within a few hours from his annual fishing trip with some friends of his from their old neighborhood in North Beach, the Little Italy section of San Francisco. She dreaded telling him that Bernie had emphatically told her he would not give her or her good-for-nothing husband a penny, and that he was seriously thinking about disinheriting her.

She was terrified what Rocco might do to her, and she wasn't sure how much longer she could hide what he did from time to time to her. Their daughter had recently asked several pointed questions about the bruises on her face and arms. Joni had lied to her about how she'd gotten the bruises. It was easier than the consequences that came from telling the truth.

She remembered how angry her father had been all those years ago when she'd told him she'd fallen in love with Rocco. Bernie had asked her what Rocco's profession was. She hadn't known at the time that he was a runner for Gino Luchese, or more precisely, for the crime family that ran the San Francisco Mafia. Rocco hadn't told her that. He'd said he worked for a man as his administrative assistant and often had to leave the house unexpectedly when something came up. It was only later that she found out the "something" usually involved drugs or money.

Many times she'd wanted out of the marriage, but Rocco had made it very clear to her that the only way she'd get out of their marriage was feet first. After several years he'd told her the only reason he'd married her was because she was Bernie Spitzer's daughter, and everyone in San Francisco knew how wealthy he was. They could hardly avoid reading about his overly generous gifts to different charities. What angered Rocco the most was that such generous gifts were never extended to Bernie's daughter and her husband.

When she'd told Bernie she was marrying Rocco, and she'd like Bernie to give her away, Bernie refused point blank. He told her a private investigator he'd hired had determined that Rocco worked for the Luchese family and was probably a part of the Italian Mafia. Joni accused Bernie of lying about it, because he didn't like Rocco. Their relationship hadn't improved with time. When Bernie refused to attend her wedding, her brother Larry had given her away. It had broken her mother's heart not to attend her only daughter's wedding, but after she'd seen the report from the private investigator, it had left little room in her mind that the report was correct. Joni wished she'd listened to her parents, but it was way too late for that now.

Joni had deliberately chosen to know as little as possible about Rocco's line of work. They were always struggling financially and many times, Rocco had told her he'd be glad when Bernie was dead, because then they'd be rich. Privately, she wasn't so sure that was going to happen. Yesterday, when she'd had lunch with her brother Larry, he'd told her he was certain Bernie was going to disinherit both of them. She didn't know what Rocco was going to say about it, and in the back of her mind, there was a nagging thought that if she couldn't produce the money Rocco had thought she could, he might think she was expendable, and in his line of work, that wasn't a term she was very anxious to explore.

"Hey, babe, your favorite Italian stallion is home," Rocco said as he came through the front door an hour later. "How about gettin' me a beer? All that talkin' and fishin' made me thirsty. So, whaddya hear from the money man? Has he had a change of heart and decided his darling lil' daughter should get an early inheritance?" Rocco greeted Joni with a lecherous pinch to her behind. She could smell the alcohol on his breath, and turned toward the refrigerator.

Rocco threw his fishing gear on the floor, and Joni knew it would stay there until she picked it up and put it away later. "Hope so," he went on, "cuz I jes' spent a bundle on a nice little deal that oughta make us a ton of money, but I gotta come up with a bunch of cash, like pronto. Tol' my friend that it might take me a little while, but I figured you could wheedle some out of your dad now that he's getting' up there in years. Tol' the guy worst case scenario is he'd have to wait until the ol' guy bit the dust. He said that wasn't a problem, and he'd take an IOU 'til ya' get yer' inheritance. So, what's up?" Rocco asked as he sat at the kitchen table drinking the beer she'd given him.

"Uhh, Rocco, I don't think that's going to happen," Joni said as she looked away from him, unable to meet his gaze. She began to pick up the things he'd thrown on the floor.

"What are ya' talkin' about?" Rocco set his beer bottle down with a bang. "This is serious, Joni. My tush is on the line with this one. I gotta have that money. Tell me the ol' man's gone and yer' gonna get the money. Heck, I'd even be okay with Larry gettin' half. I mean, who's the ol' guy gonna leave it to? That bimbo girlfriend of his that's young enough to be his granddaughter? Fat chance, as much as he likes his money."

"I had lunch with Larry yesterday," Joni said quietly, her timid voice trembling. "He told me he talked to dad recently, and he's threatening to disinherit Larry and me. From what he said, there's not going to be any early money for me, and there may not be any money at all, even after he's gone." Joni held her breath, waiting for Rocco to erupt.

"Ain't gonna happen," Rocco sneered. "Gimme another beer. Joni, I need that money, and I got friends that'll make sure I get it. I've been holdin' off doin' anything, thinkin' we could get it the nice and easy way, but it looks like that ain't gonna happen. This deal I'm in is so sweet I'd sacrifice my own mother if she could get me the money, but she can't. The only person who can get me the money is yer' dad." He took a slug from the bottle Joni had just handed him. "Tell you what, sweetheart, I'll take over from here. You ain't done that good a job handlin' it on yer' own. Ya' asked me to stay out of it and I have, but those days are over. I got friends that know how to take care of problems like this, if you know what I mean."

Joni began to sort a pile of laundry. Rocco's dirty things caused her to hold her breath. "I don't think I want to know about this, Rocco."

"Nice to know we can agree on somethin' at last. Ya' won't know a thing, but ya' better start thinkin' about what yer' gonna do with the money that'll soon be comin' yer' way," he said as he stood up from the kitchen table. "I'm goin' outside. Need to make a few calls, and it'd be better if ya' didn't know nothin'."

Joni had lived with Rocco for almost thirty years and knew that once his mind was made up, there was no room for compromise. She never expected her father to be on the short end of a no compromise situation.

CHAPTER EIGHT

"If you'd care to, why don't you tell me about yourself, Michelle?" Liz said, as they sat in Gertie's diner. "All I know is that a man you're seeing called one of my husband's law partners and asked him to book a stay for you. I'm always interested in who comes to the spa and why."

Michelle looked away for a few moments and then turned back to Liz. "I suppose I'm like a lot of other people in that I occasionally need a little vacation from life."

"That's a rather provocative statement," Liz said. "Care to tell me more? I'm not prying, just interested." She took a sip of her milkshake and watched Michelle, who was gazing absently off into space.

"Sure, I have nothing to hide." Michelle gave Liz a tight smile. "The short story is that I'm in love with a man who has no interest in getting married. Period. He treats me very well and pays for everything, way beyond what I need, so I really have no complaints."

"Okay, that's the short story. We have time and if you care to, how about telling me the long version of your story? The hamburgers take a little time and as busy as it is in here, Gertie won't be joining us."

After a moment, Michelle said, "I imagine my story isn't all that different from a lot of other women, although maybe my path to adulthood was a little more stressful than that of a lot of them." She hesitated before continuing. "You see, I never knew my parents. My mother dropped me off on some church steps when I was a newborn. From then until I was sixteen, the people I grew up with were a revolving door of foster families. Some were good, some not so good. The not so good got a bit more pronounced as I developed into womanhood. Several of the foster fathers took a special interest in me, if you know what I mean." Looking away from Liz, Michelle clutched her napkin.

"Oh, Michelle, I'm so sorry. No child should have to be placed in environments like that," Liz said reaching across the table and putting her hand over Michelle's. She was thinking of her children, Brittany and Jonah, who had been raised by Liz and her husband, Joe, in a loving household. Fortunately, the children were adults when he suffered a fatal heart attack and although they grieved, they weren't in their formative years.

Michelle looked at Liz's hand on hers. "I guess I spent the next years looking for the love I never got as a child because I managed to marry three men and divorce three men," she said sadly. "The only good thing that came of it was that my last husband was a wealthy banker, and when I unexpectedly discovered him and our maid in a compromising situation, his divorce settlement to me was very generous. Funny enough, I was just settling the last details of our divorce in your husband's law office, when I ran, literally, into Bernie, the man I've been with for several years."

"I didn't realize that you'd been a client at the law office. My husband told me it was Bernie who called his partner."

"I doubt if there was any reason your husband would know about it. Sometimes I feel like a cartoon character gone bad or some joke in a novel. You see, Bernie is eighty-three and as I mentioned, has no intention of getting married to me or anyone else, and I understand why. He's been a widower for twenty-five years and has two ne'er-do-well children. I've wanted to have his baby for a long time, because I really love him, and let's face it, my biological clock is ticking. He's always said he didn't want another child. A few days ago, my doctor suggested that Bernie donate his sperm to a sperm bank, and I would be the one authorized to use it if I still wanted a baby after he died."

Liz noticed that Michelle's lip was quivering, and it was several moments before the younger woman had composed herself enough to continue.

"Bernie agreed to do it." She raised her head up and smiled wryly at Liz. "I think it was more to shut me up than anything else, but it is something for me to think about, although even with his advancing years, that would probably be a long time off in the future. As a matter of fact, my clock will probably have run out by then. Anyway, that's kind of who I am and where I came from."

"Do you have any family that you're aware of?" Liz asked.

"No. I have no one. There's simply me, myself, and I. When Bernie dies, I don't really know where I'll go or what I'll do. He's been wonderful to me for the last few years, and although I know he's completely against marriage, he loves me, and he's shown it in a number of ways. When he's not around, I'll be completely alone." She looked down at her hands, and her hair fell across her face. Liz saw a tear trickle down her cheek.

"Michelle, I know we've just met, but I feel like we have a connection. I don't want to be presumptuous, but if you ever need a friend, or even someone you'd like to think of as a sister, I'd be honored if you'd give me a call. I have no idea where this is coming from, but it just feels right to me. What do you say?"

Michelle wiped her cheek with the red paper napkin. "Liz, I can't think of anything that would make me happier. I have to admit that I often feel so terribly alone. Thank you. Hopefully, if I ever need to call on you, it will be a long time away, but it's so reassuring to know that I have someone in my court. Again, thank you."

There's an old saying that when man makes plans, God laughs. On that particular day, God was definitely laughing.

CHAPTER NINE

Dr. Jerome Throckmorton, or Dr. "T" as his loving patients called him, looked longingly at the photograph of the woman in the bikini that was on his screensaver. She hadn't come cheap. Women who were beautiful and trying to make it in the movies always came with a heavy price tag, but it was a price he'd gladly paid. He knew every time he went anywhere with Lupe, grown men became slobbering idiots at the sight of her, and women instantly hated her.

He understood exactly how those men felt, because he'd been one of them. There had been no reason for his spur-of-the-moment trip to Cabo San Lucas, other than his third divorce had just become final, and he was glad to get rid of his burdensome wife, although the hefty amount of alimony her attorney had managed to get for her would keep him busy delivering babies for a long time. But when he saw Lupe, whatever the circumstances were that had led up to their meeting on the beach, it was worth it. Skin the color of caramel, the largest brown eyes he'd ever seen, a shiny mane of dark black hair that a man could get lost in, and a bikini that barely covered a body that was meant for one thing – pleasure. He instantly knew he had to have her.

He remembered calling his office manager and telling her something had come up, and he had to take some extra time off from his busy ob-gyn medical practice. He'd spent the time off convincing Lupe that while the movies were intriguing, her chances of making it big were minimal, and that as his wife he would give her everything she'd ever want. Lupe was no fool. The old saying "A bird in the hand is worth two in the bush" made her think twice about her future, and along with a little, no, a lot of urging from Dr. T, she was on the plane with him as his wife when he returned to San Francisco ten days later.

Sometimes you make a deal with the devil, and Dr. T's part of the deal was to keep her in the manner to which she wanted to become accustomed, no matter what the cost. In the year since they'd become man and wife it seemed like he and his bookkeeper were meeting almost hourly about his financial situation which was becoming more dismal by the day. Lupe had completely ensnared him, and there was no way he was going to tell her he couldn't afford to buy her whatever she wanted. The answer to this dilemma was that he had to find a way to get more money.

Shortly after he'd returned from Mexico, he'd read about a new California law that had been enacted regarding women who had artificially conceived a child using the sperm of a donor who had previously died. Apparently the new law was needed, because a number of military servicemen who had been assigned to dangerous combat tours of duty, and weren't sure whether they'd make it back alive.

They'd donated their sperm to a sperm bank so their wives could have their children in the event of their death. In such circumstances, under the terms of the new law, the deceased father was deemed the parent of the newborn child, even though the child had been conceived after the father was deceased. Privately, he thought that was kind of strange, but from the number of women who had taken advantage of the law, he realized he was in the minority.

The new law further provided that such a child was entitled to all of the same legal benefits as an heir of the deceased father's estate in spite of the fact that the child was neither conceived nor born until after the father's death. Dr. T realized that having a sperm bank business in conjunction with his medical practice would be a natural, and so it had proven to be. It had certainly helped to pay the huge bills Lupe had mindlessly incurred, but he was still in a constant state of not being able to balance his finances.

When Michelle D'Amato had come to his office that afternoon for her annual examination and told him how much she wanted to have a child by the man she was seeing, light bulbs began going off in his head, and he knew he might have the answer to his financial plight.

She'd mentioned that the man's name was Bernie Spitzer. Like practically anyone in San Francisco who read the papers or listened to the news, Dr. T. was well aware of who Bernie Spitzer was. He was also well aware of the vast fortune Bernie Spitzer had amassed. It wasn't a large leap to think that if Michelle could convince Bernie to donate his sperm enabling her to have his child after he was deceased, Dr. T. could use it as leverage to get some of the money that Bernie's child would be entitled to, and which Michelle would control. He didn't think $500,000 would be an unreasonable sum to expect, and it certainly would make his life a lot easier.

The only problem was that Bernie Spitzer was alive, he was healthy, and he wasn't showing any signs of being eligible for admission to a mortuary anytime soon.

Well, sometimes for things to happen, they need a little help, Dr. T decided, and this might be one of those times.

Funny how opportune life can sometimes be, like having Michelle come to his office and giving him the opportunity to solve all of his financial problems. He hadn't wasted any time telling her how happy he'd be to take care of everything if she could convince Bernie to come see him. Having been Michelle's doctor for several years, he was certain she'd be able to do her part, and then the rest would be up to him.

CHAPTER TEN

"I understand from the owner of our favorite diner that you and Michelle went there for lunch today. How did you get along with her?" Roger asked as he walked into the kitchen at the Red Cedar Lodge.

"Absolutely great. She's got quite a life story," Liz said as she handed him a glass of wine. "Sit down, and I'll tell you about it."

When she'd finished, he looked at her and said, "Kind of makes you thankful you didn't have to go through what she's had to endure. I admire her for doing so well, although it sounds like she regrets not having had a stable marriage or children."

"Definitely." Liz took a sip of her wine. "But looking at where she came from, I'd say she's done quite well for herself. I really liked her. I don't know why, but for some reason, I felt a strong bond with her. I'd love to see her again, but it's pretty rare that I ever see a guest once they leave the spa. I just wish her well."

"From what Walter tells me, she's managed to land one of the wealthiest men in San Francisco, even if she isn't married to him. I guess monetarily he treats her like a queen. I asked Walter if she was going to inherit some of his wealth when he died, and he told me that Bernie Spitzer was his only legal failure."

"That's a term I've not heard you ever use. I've heard of bad judges, unfair verdicts, and things like that, but a legal failure? Why?"

"Evidently Bernie is worth a fortune. Walter said he'd been trying to get Bernie to set up a trust or at least a will, for quite a while. He said the last time they met Bernie walked out of his office and said he was through with all of that. Said he'd be dead when the wrangling over his estate started, and he'd let Walter earn his money."

"So, am I correct in assuming because he hasn't set up a trust or a will that Michelle will get nothing when he dies?"

Roger nodded. "That's correct. I said the same thing to Walter and he told me that other than the jewelry, the condominium, and the car Bernie has given her, she wouldn't inherit anything. He'd tried to make that clear to Bernie, but Bernie had said he'd given her plenty of cash over the last few years, and if she'd been smart, she should have invested it. Walter asked him if she had, and Bernie said he didn't know. That was the end of that."

"Wow. Seems kind of cold after a mutually loving relationship that's lasted for several years." Liz wondered if part of the earlier sadness she'd sensed from Michelle was due to the fact that Bernie didn't seem to care what happened to her after he was dead.

"Yeah, I agree, but on the other hand you have to look at what he's been through. He spent millions in legal fees during the time the hostile takeover was a threat to his company and millions more when the papers had to be drawn up for the sale of his company. Walter also said he's spent a bundle of money in attorney's fees for various things he's had to bail his son out of. Sounds to me like he's just sick of dealing with money other than enjoying it, and in some ways, I can understand his position. I don't anticipate having that problem, but I understand."

"Poor Michelle. Somehow it doesn't seem fair that she'll be left out in the cold, so to speak, when he dies. It seems to me that Bernie should have done something for her."

*****

"Michelle, you look terrific," Bernie said as she walked into his condominium after returning to San Francisco from the Red Cedar Lodge and Spa. "Evidently the few days you spent at the spa agreed with you. Would I be right?"

"Yes, it was wonderful, and I really liked the owner, Liz. We went to lunch one day and it seemed like the two of us really connected. I'd like to see her again, but I know it was probably just one of those moment in time things."

"Yes, those things happen. Here, try this," he said as he handed her a glass of Blanc De Blancs Le Mesnil-Sur-Oger 2002. "I just opened it to celebrate your return. My wine consultant said it's one of the best champagnes that has ever been made and, trust me, it wasn't cheap, but you're worth it. Let's toast to your spa excursion."

"This is wonderful, Bernie," she said as she took a sip. "Your consultant certainly knows his wine."

"For what I pay him, he should, but I look at it as a good investment, plus I have the luxury of opening whatever bottle appeals to me whenever I want. You can't actually taste many investments, which is probably why I've chosen to collect wine."

"I missed you, Bernie." Michelle stepped closer to Bernie and kissed him on the lips. "It's good to be back here with you."

"Me too, Michelle. By the way, you'll be happy to know that I got in touch with your doctor, and if you ever decide to have our child when I'm gone, a part of me is in his sperm bank. I have to tell you that as good as I feel, I think you'll be well past the age of childbearing when I go." He winked at her and grinned.

"That would be a very good reason not to ever have a child, Bernie. Let's toast to your continued good health and longevity," Michelle said smiling as she lightly touched the rim of her champagne flute to his.

CHAPTER ELEVEN

One morning, about four months after Michelle had been a guest at the Red Cedar Lodge and Spa, Liz's cell phone rang. "Hello. This is Liz Lucas. Is that you, Michelle? Your name popped up on my screen."

"Liz, I'm so sorry to bother you," the voice at the other end said. Liz sensed she was crying.

"Michelle, what's wrong?"

"Oh, Liz, everything is wrong. I don't know where to begin."

"I have no idea what you're talking about, but why don't you start by telling me everything that's gone on since you left the spa. I've thought about you often the last few months."

"Well, I might as well get the two biggest ones out first. Bernie's dead, and I'm pregnant."

"Good grief, Michelle. You're right. Those are huge. When did he die?"

"It happened a couple of weeks after I came back from your spa. I went up to his penthouse, you know he bought me a condominium two floors below his, and when he didn't answer the doorbell, I let myself in. He was a private man, and although he'd given me a key, I always rang the bell twice, and he'd immediately open the door. This time there was no answer. I called out, but he didn't answer, and since we had plans to go to a charity dinner for one of the organizations he supported, I was surprised when he didn't greet me."

"Oh, Michelle, I'm so sorry. So, I guess where this is leading is that you were the one to find him."

"Yes. He was dressed in his tuxedo, so he was definitely planning on going to the gala, but when I found him he was lying on the floor. I tried to administer CPR, but it was too late. I called 911. When the police and the paramedics came, all heck broke loose. The police questioned me for a long time. I finally told them I wasn't going to answer any more of their questions without my attorney being present. Bernie always told me that having an attorney at your side when dealing with the police, or anyone who might be an adversary, was critical."

"Do you have an attorney?" Liz asked.

"Only the one who handled my divorces, but fortunately I didn't need one."

"Why?"

"The police told me I could go. They said given his age and with no visible signs of trauma to his body, he probably died from natural causes."

"Michelle, I've been involved in a couple of murder cases, and usually an autopsy is performed. Did the coroner perform one?"

"No. When he came, he said there had been three homicides that night in the Tenderloin District as well as a ten-car accident on the Goslden Gate bridge. Evidently several people died in the accident. Anyway, he said with no visible signs of trauma, he was going to sign off on the death certificate and indicate Bernie's death was due to natural causes." She started to cry again.

"Michelle, take your time. I'm here for as long as you want to talk to me."

"Thank you. Give me just a moment." She was quiet for several minutes then she resumed speaking. "When I got back from the spa, Bernie told me he'd been to Dr. Throckmorton, my doctor who also owns a sperm bank, and that if I wanted to have a child by artificial insemination, he'd authorized that I could, but only after he was deceased."

"And that's how you got pregnant?"

"Yes. I waited two months, and they were the worst two months of my life. Sure, I know a lot of people, but I really don't have any close friends, and as I told you, I have no family that I'm aware of."

"Did Bernie have children? If he did, maybe they could be your family? Surely you could share your mutual grief."

"Bernie has two ne'er-do-well children. Those are his words, not mine. They were somewhat estranged from him, and I know he'd been thinking about disinheriting them. I guess he died before he got around to it. At least that's what his attorney, Walter Highsmith, told me. He's my attorney now."

"He's the one who called Roger and recommended the spa, isn't he? Why do you need an attorney?"

"The answer to your first question is yes. The answer to your second question is somewhat complicated."

Liz glanced at the screen of her phone. "Michelle, I see that my husband is trying to call me. I better take it. I'm supposed to meet him in the city this evening, and we were planning to spend the night in San Francisco. There may have been a change in plans. Let me take his call, and I'll get right back to you."

"No problem. I have a doctor's appointment this afternoon. I get to see the baby for the first time because Dr. T is going to do a sonogram, and I'm really excited to see him or her. Other than that, I don't have anywhere to go and nothing to do but let this baby grow, so I'll be here," she said as she ended the call.

CHAPTER TWELVE

"Hi, Roger, has there been a change in plans for tonight?"

"No, but I just talked to Walter Highsmith, and he wants to meet with me this afternoon. He told me that Bernie Spitzer died recently, and there are some complications concerning his death. I guess he died of natural causes, but I thought you'd want to know because of your relationship with Michelle. Somehow I must have missed it in the papers."

"It's ironic that you'd call with that information just now. You won't believe it, but I was just talking to Michelle on the phone when you called. I had no idea. Do you know what Walter wants to talk to you about?"

"No. The only thing he mentioned was that I might have a new client."

"Did he mean Michelle? And if he did, I wonder why, since your area of expertise is criminal defense."

"I have no idea, but I just wanted to let you know I might be a few minutes late. Rather than meet me at the restaurant, why don't you come to my office and wait here? Hate to have to fight my way through a bunch of guys sitting at your dinner table if I'm late. I'm told that's what happens when attractive women eat alone."

"Flattery will get you anywhere, love. Thanks for the compliment, but I think those days have long gone by, if they even were. I'll go to your office and wait for you. I told Michelle I'd call her back, so I may have some information for you."

After ending her call with Roger, Liz promptly called Michelle back. "I'm sorry, Michelle, but there was a change in plans for tonight, so it was a good thing I took the call." She didn't mention that Walter Highsmith had requested a meeting with Roger. "I had to leave our conversation before you had a chance to tell me why you needed an attorney."

"Liz, this whole thing has become surreal. Walter called me and told me it would probably be a good thing if I returned the key I had to Bernie's condominium. He asked if I could come to his office. We agreed on a time and I met with him. While I was there I mentioned that I was pregnant with Bernie's baby, but I wasn't sure how I was going to make ends meet. I told him, which he knew, that Bernie had bought my condominium, given me my car, and a lot of very nice jewelry along with some money, but since I was pregnant, I couldn't work. My doctor told me that getting pregnant at my age was going to require that I be very careful not to overdo things. He recommended that I spend a lot of time just resting."

"I've always heard the same thing about mothers who are a bit older the first time they're pregnant."

"I've been a model pregnant woman, but the lack of money was really worrying me. Bernie had paid my health insurance for the year, but the baby was going to be born after that, and even though I've invested the money Bernie had given me over the years, I knew I was going to be strapped for cash at some point. My doctor's the doctor for all the VIP people in San Francisco and he doesn't come cheap. I'd been in touch with the jeweler who had sold Bernie the pieces of jewelry he'd given me, but he told me I could only expect to get about fifty percent of what Bernie had paid for them."

Liz sighed and said, "I wish I could say I was surprised, but I'm not. I've heard the same thing about a new car once it's driven off of the car dealer's lot. It sure doesn't seem fair."

"No, it doesn't, but I guess that's just the way it is. Anyway, I told all that to Walter, and he said that since I was pregnant with Bernie's child, not only was the child entitled to a share of his estate, Walter could go to court and petition the court for a family allowance. In other words, the baby and I are eligible to get living expenses while I'm pregnant."

"Michelle, this sounds like something out of a movie or a novel. Did you do that?"

"Yes, evidently the courts have something in place for situations like this that require a fast court date, and Walter and I went to court ten days ago. Bernie's children, through their attorney, strongly opposed the judge's ruling when he granted me $10,000 a month, contingent on a DNA test, for the duration of my pregnancy."

"I've heard it can take months for one of those tests. How did Walter handle that?"

"He told the judge we would pay a private DNA testing company to get the results to the court within 48 hours. The report was delivered to the judge, and Bernie was declared to be the baby's father without a shadow of a doubt. Bernie's children, as his heirs, became co-administrators of his estate and hired their own attorney. He had them cut a check for $10,000 and gave it to Walter."

"Who is the opposing attorney?" Liz asked. "I'll have to ask Roger if he knows him."

"His name is Darren Michaels. Evidently, he's with a large downtown law firm. I'm sure your husband has probably heard of him. Walter told me he has a good reputation."

"Michelle, let's back up. I thought you said something about the baby being entitled to a share of Bernie's estate. How is that possible?"

"I only know what Walter told me. I guess some recent law went into effect that was designed to help women who became pregnant after their husband died in combat. The original intent of it was so the baby would be allowed to have the rights to armed services' benefits and insurance. Walter told me that even though Bernie and I had nothing to do with the military, the law specified that a child conceived after the father died was entitled to inherit all or a portion of the estate as an heir-at-law of the deceased father. The new law isn't limited to just military servicemen, but applies to everyone."

"Michelle, correct me if I'm wrong, but based on the little I know about Bernie Spitzer, that could be a huge amount. Is that right?"

"Yes. Bernie's estate is estimated to be worth around three hundred million dollars. Walter tells me after the baby's born he'll petition the probate court to have one-third of whatever the estate is valued at distributed to my baby. I guess it means my baby will be well taken care of financially. The other two-thirds of Bernie's estate will go to his two adult children. They're the neer-do-wells I told you about."

"That's wonderful news. I'm so happy for you. It looks like everything has worked out for you. I guess I'm surprised you were crying when you called me."

"Well, the problem is, I haven't told you everything, Liz. Before I called you, I'd just received a telephone call from Walter telling me that a police detective had gotten in touch with him regarding Bernie's death. He said Bernie's children had asked that the investigation concerning their father's death be re-opened. Walter suspects it's in retaliation for the $10,000 per month family allowance the judge allowed. They're accusing me of murdering their father, my baby's father," she said as she sobbed.

"That's horrible, Michelle. Why would they do that? I mean, there's plenty of money to go around."

"Not in their eyes. They want it all. Bernie told me his son had a drug problem and rehabs had been a revolving door in his life. He also said he was the ultimate sucker for any get-rich scheme that came along. I guess Bernie bailed him out a lot of times, and his daughter's husband has Mafia ties. Bernie refused to even attend her wedding, and from the little he told me, their relationship hasn't gotten any better over the years."

"What happens now?" Liz asked.

"I have a meeting with Walter this afternoon. The final reason I called is that Walter thinks I should hire your husband to defend me, if it comes to that."

Liz was quiet for several moments, then she said, "When Roger called he said Walter had requested a meeting with him. He didn't mention anything about you."

"That I don't know, but as soon as I heard it was your husband he wanted me to hire, I thought of you. Liz, I know you said you cared for me, but I don't think I can go through this alone. I'm scared I might lose Bernie's baby because of the stress. I know I'm asking an awful lot, but could you attend the meeting today? And if I am charged with murder, can you help me? I know you've been involved in solving other murders. Please, Liz, I don't have anyone else I can turn to."

Liz heard the sound of Michelle crying softly on the other end of the phone. She took a deep breath and said, "I don't know what I can do, if anything, but yes, I'll be there for you. I was planning on meeting Roger in his office following the meeting, but I'll just attend the meeting instead. Where should I meet you?"

"Let's meet in the lobby at 4:30 this afternoon. We can go up to Walter's office together and Liz, I can never thank you enough for this. Forgive me for asking for your help, but I have to do everything I can to make sure Bernie's baby is protected in every way. I'll see you this afternoon." Michelle ended the call, the sound of her anguish staying with Liz for some time afterwards.

Liz spent the next few hours getting ready for the evening meal at the lodge. She wrote notes out for Gina and did the prep work. The weather had turned cold, and she figured if she liked a warm soup on a cold day, the guests would as well. One of her favorites was a Swedish recipe a friend had given her for split pea soup with sausage, an unusual combination, but one that turned out to be delicious. She decided a Caesar salad and a loaf of warm bread would go well with it. For dessert she decided on warm baked apples with a scoop of ice cream on top.

After she'd done everything she could to help Gina prepare the meal, she gave in to Winston's big brown eyes, which seemed to be silently asking for some time with her in the form of a walk. "Okay, Winston, this is a good time. Let's take a walk around the area and give you a little exercise. Roger and I will be gone tonight, but your favorite aunt, Bertha, insists that you and Brandy Boy stay with her, and I know how much you like that."

Since she was on her own property, and Winston obeyed every command she'd ever given him, there was no reason to put a leash on him. They walked out the door, stepped over Brandy Boy, who was in his usual position of being sound asleep on the porch, and spent the next hour simply enjoying the late fall afternoon.

CHAPTER THIRTEEN

Promptly at 4:30, Liz saw Michelle walk through the front door of the law office building. "Michelle," she said as she hugged her and then pushed her away to look at her, "I didn't think it was possible, but if anything, you're even more beautiful than you were when you came to the spa. Obviously, being pregnant agrees with you." Michelle's skin was radiant, her eyes bright despite a hint of redness which made Liz suspect that she'd been crying. Her hair had grown longer, so that it fell below her shoulders and was swept back in a loose knot.

"Thank you, Liz. It's so good to see you. I shouldn't have waited so long to call you, but I'm so glad I finally did. I just didn't want to worry you or be a burden."

"Sweetheart, I wish you had, but I'm here now, and whatever I can do to make this horrible situation better, I will. I'm not talking about the baby situation, I'm talking about the sibling situation. You do realize that the baby you're carrying, whether it's a boy or a girl, will be a half-sister or half-brother to Bernie's other children."

"I do, but I've taken a vow that when Bernie looks down from above, he'll always be proud of this child of his that I'm carrying."

"That's a good attitude to take." With that said, they got in the elevator, and Michelle punched the button for the twelfth floor.

"How did the doctor's visit go? Were you able to see the baby on the sonogram?"

Michelle smiled secretively. "It was wonderful. I'll wait to tell all three of you the good news."

"That's a provocative statement, if I've ever heard one," Liz said as they got off the elevator. They walked down the hall to Walter's office, and Michelle gave their names to the receptionist.

"Mr. Hightower told me you should go directly to his office when you arrived, Ms. D'Amato. I believe you know where it is," the receptionist said. "I'll call him and let him know you're here."

Michelle and Liz walked down the hall towards Walter's office. Liz had been in the law firm's offices several times, first when her late husband, Joe, had died and his attorney was probating his estate. She'd also met Roger several times at his office before they attended business functions or had dinner in San Francisco. Even though Liz loved Red Cedar, there was something about San Francisco's energy, the cable cars, the museums, the restaurants, and everything else the city offered, that still sang a siren song to her. There were few businesses in Red Cedar that could afford or would even think to hang exquisite pieces of art on the walls of the hall like the ones the law firm had on display.

When they entered Walter's office, Liz immediately heard Roger say, "Liz, what are you doing here?"

Liz smiled at her husband and said, "It's a long story, and one that I think will be interesting."

A bear of a man with a healthy head of silver hair who looked like he could have been part of the famous San Francisco hippie movement and the Summer of Love, stepped from behind a large desk and said, "I'm sorry. I don't think I've had the pleasure of meeting you, but judging from Roger's greeting, you must be Liz, his wife. I'm Walter Highsmith." He held out his hand and shook hers.

"Walter," Michelle said, "I took the liberty of asking Liz to join me. I knew you wouldn't mind, and quite frankly, I need some moral support."

"Uhh, I kind of feel like the odd man out," Roger said. "I have no clue why I'm here, who this woman is, and why my wife is here. Walter, you're the one who asked me to meet with you. Want to throw me a lifeline?"

"Ladies, please be seated," Walter said indicating several club chairs surrounding a coffee table at the far end of the room next to expansive floor-to-ceiling windows that overlooked the city, San Francisco Bay, and the Golden Gate Bridge.

"Roger, I'd like to introduce you to Michelle D'Amato. She was a guest at your wife's spa, but evidently you didn't have a chance to meet her. Michelle, this is Roger Langley, Liz's husband." The two of them shook hands. "Roger, I believe I told you that Bernie Spitzer died a few months ago." Roger nodded. "There's more to it than that." Walter told him about Michelle's pregnancy, the probate of Bernie's estate, and the recent court appearance to obtain a family support order for Michelle's unborn baby."

"Thanks for the background, Walter, but I still don't know what any of that has to do with me."

"I'm getting there, Roger. I had a telephone call this morning from a police detective I've known for many years, Mitch Latham. When Michelle was questioned after she discovered Bernie's body at his condominium, she told the police she wouldn't answer any more questions without her attorney being present. She gave them my name because over the years I'd met her several times when she'd come to the office with Bernie.

"Mitch wanted to alert me to the fact that Bernie's children, Joni and Larry, had asked the police department to reopen the investigation file concerning their father's death. They said they'd like the department to look at Michelle as a suspect, because now that she's pregnant with Bernie's child, she had a lot to gain by his death.

The reason I wanted to meet with you and Michelle was so she could hire you in the event she's charged with Bernie's murder. According to law, the baby she's carrying will inherit one-third of Bernie's estate, and his children think that provides a very good motive for murdering their father. The detective thought the department might agree with them."

Michelle interrupted him. "Walter, I just found out today that I'm not carrying a baby, as you phrased it, my doctor has confirmed that I'm carrying twins. I'm not a math person, but it seems to me that the babies will inherit one-half of Bernie's estate, rather than the one-third you mentioned. Am I right?"

Liz, Walter, and Roger looked at her in stunned silence. Walter was the first to recover. "Michelle, Bernie's estate is thought to be in the area of around three hundred million. That means the two babies will receive seventy-five million each, and what's disturbing to me as an attorney, is that his present children will likewise share the other half, with each of them receiving seventy-five million. Because of your pregnancy, first with one child and now with two, you've essentially just cut each of their inheritances to one-fourth instead of one-half. When they find that out they're going to go ballistic. We're going to have to go back to court and request more family support. I can almost guarantee you that you will become a strong suspect if it's determined Bernie was murdered. Roger, what do you think?"

Roger was quiet for several moments, and then he began to speak. "I've never encountered a situation like this. I'm going to talk off the top of my head, but I'll also need to do some research if you choose to hire me, Michelle."

"I do. Draw up the papers, and I'll sign them. I want you to handle everything to clear my name," Michelle instructed him. "Let me make this crystal clear. I loved Bernie more than anything in the world, and I had nothing to do with his death. Absolutely nothing." She looked first at Roger and then at Walter. "Doesn't the fact that the police and the coroner could find no signs of trauma on his body indicate that he died from natural causes? That's what the coroner said when he came to Bernie's condo on the night he died."

"This is my area, Walter, so let me respond," Roger said. "Michelle, you are perfectly correct in that assumption, however, under certain circumstances a body may be exhumed and an autopsy performed when there is reason to believe there is justifiable cause for doing so. In this case, I don't think his children will have a problem getting a judge to order that the body be exhumed and an autopsy conducted. What I would suggest is that we proceed under the assumption that you will be a suspect, and if the autopsy findings indicate murder, there is a good chance you will be charged with murder. I'm sorry, but I want to be honest with you."

"Michelle, Roger is just telling you the worst case scenario," Liz said, noticing that Michelle had visibly paled as Roger was talking. "I think the best thing to do is have Roger and Walter ask you all the questions the police and/or anyone else will ask, and then be done with it. Since you're hiring Roger, he can do all the talking for you from this time forward. You told me before that you need to have as little drama in your life as possible, or words to that effect. Let them take care of the forthcoming drama and finger pointing."

"I can't believe any of this is happening," Michelle said in a sad tone of voice. "It's not fair for the happiest time of my life to be overshadowed by the threat of going to prison for a murder I didn't commit. What will happen to my babies?' Her voice cracked. "I don't have anyone who can take care of them. I don't want them to end up like me, in and out of different foster homes, and being abused. If I ever thought they would be subjected to that sort of life, I never would have gotten pregnant."

"Michelle, Roger has to do everything he can before any problems arise. That way he'll be fully prepared to do whatever is necessary to make sure you come out of this as a free woman. You owe it to those babies to do your part. Yes, this is traumatic, and no one would suggest it isn't, but it needs to be done. After this evening, we'll do all the heavy lifting. The only thing that will probably be required by you is to answer a couple of questions in court regarding the increase in family allowance and whatever the detective will ask you. Keep in mind, I'll be with you in court, and Roger will be with you if and when his role as a defense attorney is needed. Think you can do that?" Walter asked.

"Yes," she said in an almost inaudible voice, tears visible in the corners of her eyes. She gratefully accepted the glass of water Liz handed her.

"Okay, I'd like to get started with where you were and what you did on the day of Bernie's death, and don't leave anything out, no matter how inconsequential you think it might be," Roger said, taking control.

For the next two hours, Michelle answered all of Roger's questions. Walter primarily listened, interjecting something once in a while. Liz noticed he seemed very concerned about his client. At one point he told everyone it was time to take a break. Liz and Roger walked into the hall and decided to go home when the meeting was over rather than spend the night in the city. Based on the events of the last couple of hours, neither one of them felt like having a good time in San Francisco.

When they walked back into Walter's office, Michelle was eating a sandwich and drinking a glass of milk. She looked up at them and said, "Can you believe it? When Walter knew I was coming into the office this afternoon, he had his secretary buy some milk and get a sandwich for me. He felt a mother-to-be should have something in her stomach. I mean, how thoughtful is that?" she asked, giving him one of her million-watt smiles.

Very thoughtful, Liz thought. *Amazingly thoughtful.* She looked over at Walter who was grinning from ear to ear and then she looked down at his left hand. No ring was on it. *Oh boy, bet I know who the stepfather of the twins is going to be. Wait until Roger hears this.*

Roger resumed his questioning and after another hour he said, "Michelle, I don't have anything else to ask you. Would you like to ask me anything?"

"No, and thank you for being so kind to me. I'm sure this wasn't easy for you." She turned to Liz and said, "Liz, I have a favor to ask of you, and it's a pretty big one."

"Of course, Michelle, I'd be happy to do whatever I can for you."

"You might not be quite so willing once you hear what it is."

"I'll bite. Try me."

"You told me the day we had lunch at Gertie's Diner that you had been involved in the attempt to solve several murders, and that you'd been successful. I know this isn't a murder investigation yet, and believe me, no one hopes more than me that it doesn't become one, but if it's determined that it is, I want to be prepared. I guess that's the wrong way to put it. After Walter called this morning, I made a list of people I thought might be considered suspects if Bernie was murdered. It seems to me if you could find a little something out about them before Bernie's body is exhumed, and I'm possibly charged with murder, we would be way ahead of the police. Please, Liz, can you help me by doing that?"

Liz looked over at Roger who made the smallest of nods with his head indicating that it was all right with him. She turned and looked at Michelle. "I'd be happy to help you if I can. I won't promise anything, and I'm not a professional, but I've been lucky in the past, and if it comes to that, maybe I'll get lucky again."

CHAPTER FOURTEEN

After agreeing to help Michelle, Liz said, "Let me see the list of suspects you've prepared."

"These three names are just people that Bernie and I talked about over the years," Michelle said, showing her the piece of paper she'd written the names on. "There may be a lot of others, and who knows, it could have been a random thing, although from what the police told me and from what I saw, nothing was taken from either Bernie or his condo, and he had a lot of things that were quite valuable. He always wore a large diamond ring and his one luxury in life, as he called it, was to buy a new Rolex watch each year. Both of those were on him when I discovered his body."

"Maybe before we get to the suspects, we should talk about some of the valuable things in his home," Walter said. "I know he collected wine. What about art, things of that nature?"

Michelle nodded at Walter. "He had a man who advised him regarding his wine collection. As you know, Walter, he bought a condominium on the floor below his penthouse so he could store his wines in different rooms at the perfect temperature required for each type of wine. I've not been in his wine collection area since he died, so I have no idea if it's still intact."

"Liz, since you're going to be doing the legwork on this part of

Michelle's problem, let me give you the key to his condominium," Walter said. "I think Roger's time should be spent working up a legal defense if it's needed, and I'm going to be involved doing the work up to petition the court for an increased family allowance and trying to make sure that Michelle's life is as stress free as possible." He gazed affectionately at Michelle, who responded with a radiant smile.

If I were a gambling person, I'd bet everything I own that Walter has far more than a business interest in Michelle, and from the way she's looking at him, I think the feeling is mutual. What a strange turn of events, Liz thought.

"Bernie had a lot of art, and I mean really good expensive art in his condo, but it was all there the night he died," Michelle continued. "I was familiar with what was on the walls and displayed on various different tables, and I don't remember seeing anything that was missing, but then again, I was in a pretty emotional state of mind, so I could have missed something."

Liz interjected, "Michelle, I hate to ask this of you, but are you up to taking a look at his condo to see if something is missing? Maybe it was a jealous collector, or an art dealer who resented his collection. I know I'm reaching for straws here, but we have to start somewhere."

"I think that's a good idea," Walter added. "Since the police haven't ruled that Bernie's death was a murder, I doubt that anyone has gone through his things. Actually, Liz, forget about the key. I told the attorney for the estate that I'd get Michelle's key to the condo back from her and give it to him tomorrow, so I think we need to go there tonight. Would that be all right with all of you?" He looked at them and each of them nodded.

"I only have a couple of names on my list, but here goes," Michelle said. "The first one is Larry Spitzer. I've told Liz about him and here's the little I know about him as related to me by Bernie," she said as she told them what she'd told Liz earlier that morning. "The second one on the list is his daughter, Joni. Again, I've never met her, and I don't know all that much about her, but here's what I do know." She proceeded to tell the other three what she knew about Bernie's younger child.

"Liz," Roger said, "You and Sean, the firm's private investigator, have a great relationship. I think you should call him first thing in the morning and see what he can find out. The first thing anyone involved in a homicide investigation looks at is who has the most to gain from the murder, and since Larry and Joni are his children and heirs to his estate, I would definitely start there. Given the fact that before Michelle became pregnant with the twins, their combined inheritance amounted to a whopping three hundred million dollars. I'd say they had a lot to gain by Bernie's death."

"I will. Sean's fabulous," Liz said as she turned to Michelle. "I've never been able to figure out how he does it, but he finds out things no one could possibly know. I definitely want to talk to him."

With an uncomfortable look on her face, Michelle spoke up and said, "Roger, you said the first thing anyone looks at is who has the most to gain, so let's not hide it. Now that I'm pregnant, my future born children, and indirectly me, have a lot to gain from Bernie's death. That makes me think I would be looked at very closely, isn't that right?"

Roger looked directly at Michelle and said, "Yes, unfortunately, you will be looked at, and very closely. I was going to tell Liz later that she should also ask Sean to do some research on you, and here's why. There is nothing worse for a criminal defense attorney than when his client withholds information from him. I'm not saying you have or would withhold anything from me, but I want to have the same information about you that the law enforcement authorities have. I hope you understand this is not personal, this is simply part of any defense attorney's work-up on a case. Please don't take offense."

"None taken, Roger. I understand, and believe me, no one wants my name cleared more than me." Michelle jutted her chin out. "I will tell you that even though I've been married three times, was shifted from one foster home to another, and did a fair amount of defending my honor from overzealous foster fathers and uncles, as they liked to be called, there is nothing in my past that I'm ashamed of. You'll find there's no criminal record or anything else that's negative about me. I've even managed to stay on good terms with my ex-husbands, which in this day and age, is something of a miracle," she added with a laugh.

"Okay, Bernie's two children are probably at the top of the list of suspects, particularly given that each of them has had financial problems and been involved in some rather grey areas. Michelle, can you think of anyone else?" Liz asked.

"There is man by the name of Jim Brown, who Bernie spoke of from time to time," Michelle offered. "Evidently he and Bernie were partners and together they founded Spitzer Electronics. Bernie told me once that he had become the sole owner of the company when he found out Jim hadn't applied for a patent for the product that was the main reason for their success. He told me when he made the discovery, he filed a patent application, and a patent was granted to Bernie in his sole name. Bernie took control of the company, paid Jim a lump sum of $100,000 as termination pay to buy him out, and told him he was no longer welcome at the company. From the way he talked about it, I think he wondered if what he had done was the right thing."

"Why do you say that?" Liz asked.

"Bernie told me that from time to time Jim wrote him asking for money, since he was living on social security and barely able to make ends meet. I think there was some guilt involved on Bernie's part because he was so wealthy, and the man who had been his partner was now destitute. Whenever Bernie mentioned it, he always laughed it off and said that was just the way things worked in the business world, but I always wondered if he was being honest. Bernie had a heart just like everyone else, but it was just hard to find sometimes."

"Do you know anything about Jim? Like where he lives?" Liz asked.

Michelle shook her head. "No, the only thing I know is that his name is Jim Brown."

"I'll ask Sean to see what he can find out about him, but Roger, something bothers me about him," Liz said, turning to her husband.

"What?" Roger asked.

"If he was Bernie's partner and he started the company with Bernie, he'd probably be somewhat elderly. I have trouble visualizing an elderly man committing murder," Liz said.

"That's somewhat true." Roger said, rubbing his chin. "The majority of homicides are committed by people who would be younger than him, but that still doesn't rule him out. If he was harboring a grudge for a number of years, he might have felt that at his advanced age he really didn't have much to lose by murdering Bernie. He might know how impacted the criminal court system is here in California and figured he'd be dead before he was ever convicted, and with some attorney filing one motion after another for new trials, etc., he'd probably be right."

"Great. So, we have Bernie's children, his former business partner, and I hate to say this, and Michelle, as possible suspects," Liz said. "I'll call Sean in the morning and see what he can find out. If we're through here, let's all go to Bernie's condominium and see if we can find anything there."

"Michelle, I'll take you in my car," Walter said. "Roger, Liz, we'll meet you there," Walter said.

CHAPTER FIFTEEN

"Good evening, Ms. D'Amato, pleasure to see you," the doorman at Bernie and Michelle's condominium building said as he opened the door for them.

"Thanks, Joe. Good to see you, too," Michelle said as the four of them walked over to the elevators. "As you know, Bernie owns the penthouse, and there's a special elevator for his unit. You need a key for it." She turned to Walter. "I completely forgot that I had it. I'll give it to you as well as the key to his penthouse." She inserted it in the lock, and they stepped into the elevator.

When the elevator doors opened and they reached the top of the building, the assembled group found themselves in a small reception area fronted by two large oak doors. Michelle inserted her key in the door lock and they walked into Bernie's penthouse. For a moment Liz, Roger, and Walter simply looked out the floor-to-ceiling windows at the stupendous view of the city. They could see the cable cars far below as well as the lights of cars on the Golden Gate Bridge. Liz doubted that there were any views of the city more impressive and stunning than those from Bernie's penthouse.

"Walter," Roger said, "why don't you and Michelle take a walk through the rooms and Michelle, since you know what was here, see if anything's missing? I'd like to go through his bedroom. People often keep important things close to them. To save time, Liz, why don't you go through his desk? Look for anything that seems unusual. If anyone has a better idea, let me know."

"Sounds good. Let's meet back here when we're finished," Walter said as he and Michelle began to walk around the living room. "See anything missing?" he asked.

"So far, nothing," she said.

Roger went down the hall to the master bedroom and began to open the drawers in Bernie's dresser and nightstands. He found what any well-dressed man would have in his drawers: socks, underwear, handkerchiefs, and things like that. He found a gun in the nightstand, but when he tried to open the chamber it was rusted shut from lack of use. He went into the closet and again, found nothing of interest other than a safe which was locked. He made a mental note to ask Michelle if she knew the combination, but other than that he found nothing that was unusual.

He heard Liz calling him from Bernie's office. "Roger, would you come here? I think I've found something." He walked down the hall to the office and found Liz sitting at Bernie's desk, an open file on the desk, and a piece of paper in her hand.

"What did you find?" he asked, as he walked up behind her.

"I found a file with a tab marked 'Jim Brown'. When I opened it, this was on the top of the file. Everything else in the file is attached with fasteners, you know, the kind where you punch holes and then secure the item to the folder. It hadn't been secured or even punched, which makes me think it's the newest item in the file."

"If your spa goes under, you can probably give Sean a run for his money as a private investigator," Roger said with a chuckle. "That's pretty good sleuthing. Have you read it?"

"Of course, and that's why I called you. It's a note with a signature by someone named Jim Brown. Actually, I think it's a threat. Here, read it for yourself, and see what you think."

Roger quickly scanned the terse note which read, *"Bernie, I'm old and I've been told I don't have much longer to live because, the big C is in me. If I were you, I'd be very careful, because it's time for me to do something I should have done long ago."*

He put the note down and looked at Liz. "I agree with you. This definitely qualifies as a threat. I want to take it to our handwriting analysis expert and see if there's a match with Jim's handwriting and signature. As I recall, Walter became Bernie's attorney because one of the partners at the law firm retired. When Bernie became the sole owner of the company and forced this Brown guy out, Brown probably had to sign some papers. Let me see what I can find out." He pulled a clear plastic baggie out of his pocket and put the note in it.

"Roger, I've been through every file in every drawer, and this was the only thing I found. Unless someone else found something that needs our attention, why don't we call it a night and drive home? I'm tired, and if I'm this worn out, I can imagine how Michelle must be feeling. Pregnancy tired is like no other kind of being tired, and that's on top of finding out she may be a murder suspect, and that she's carrying twins. That's a lot for one day."

"I couldn't agree more. Let's go back to the living room and say our goodbyes. Fortunately, Michelle only has to go down two floors to be home, and I'm sure Walter will make sure she gets there safely."

Michelle and Walter were sitting in the living room, quietly talking. They looked up when Roger said, "We did find a note, so all is not lost." He took it out of the plastic baggie he'd put it in and handed it to Walter to read while Michelle looked over his shoulder.

"It doesn't make him the murderer," Walter said, raising an eyebrow, "but I think he's a bona fide qualifier for the role of suspect, don't you?" He handed the note back to Roger.

"Absolutely," Roger answered. "Walter, when Bernie became your client, what happened to his previous files?"

"They're in a file cabinet in my office. Why?"

"I would think there would have been some paperwork regarding the company when Bernie forced this Brown guy to leave. If Bernie had been my client, I would have made sure that Brown signed something about not having any further rights to the company. Any chance you could get your secretary to see if she could find the documents involved in that transaction? If she can, would you have her bring it to my office? I want to have our handwriting analysis expert look at the papers and this note and see if the writing and the signatures match."

"I'll have her do it as soon as she gets in the office tomorrow. You should have it no later than ten." He looked over at Michelle, whose eyes were drooping. "Roger, Liz, I hope you don't mind, but I think I better get my client home. Looks like the babies need a nap and for sure their mother does."

"Michelle, before you go, I have a question," Roger said. "I found a safe in Bernie's closet. Do you know anything about it?"

"Only that it didn't work. Bernie often said it was the biggest waste of money he'd ever spent. He said he'd never been able to get it open, and he'd long ago forgotten the combination. He told me he'd never even gotten a chance to put anything in it."

"Sounds like that's a dead end. Liz and I are ready to leave. Is that okay with you?" Roger asked.

"It's fine. I'll use Michelle's key to lock the door on our way out, and tomorrow I'll courier the front door key and the elevator key over to Darren Michaels. Have a safe drive, and Roger, I'll talk to you tomorrow. Liz, nice to meet you, but I would have preferred that it was under different circumstances," Walter said, standing up and putting out his hand to help Michelle out of her chair.

"Liz, thank you for everything," Michelle said. "I really don't think I could have gotten through today without your help. I guess the only thing I can do now is wait for one of you to call me."

Liz walked over to Michelle and gave her a big hug. "Try not to worry, Michelle. I know you have the best defense attorney available at your disposal and from what I'm seeing, I think you're in very safe hands with Walter."

"Yes, I am," Michelle said as she turned and smiled at Walter who had a silly grin on his face and looked like he'd just picked all the winning horses in the superfecta at Golden Gate Fields.

CHAPTER SIXTEEN

"Well, Mr. Defense Attorney, what did you think about all of that?" Liz asked as they began the drive back to the Red Cedar Lodge and Spa. "Actually, hold the thought. I want to call Bertha and alert her that we're going to be home tonight, so she won't be alarmed when she sees lights on. I'm glad I had the house built on the property for her and her husband. As hard as she works, when it's time to go home, now all she has to do is to take a couple of steps and she's home. Of course, the bonus is that it frees us up, because she keeps Winston and Brandy Boy when we're away from the lodge, and Winston loves to spend time with her. I have this feeling they let him up on their bed. I just hope he doesn't get used to it."

"He can't get used to it if we don't allow it, and I think that dog is smart enough to know when he can get by with something and when he can't. I wouldn't worry about it," Roger said as they sped along, his eyes looking straight ahead at the road.

Liz completed the call to Bertha and then said, "Okay, Roger, back to business. I'll resume where I left off a couple of minutes ago. What are your thoughts about everything?"

"I'm processing them, so if I'm a little slow to speak, bear with me. There's so much going on here, it's hard to isolate one thought. Let me start with the fact that Bernie could have been murdered. I think it's a definite possibility. I've seen a couple of other cases where an elderly person died and no autopsy was conducted for the very reason one wasn't conducted in this case, no signs of trauma. But when someone is that wealthy, you'd think it would be mandatory." Roger looked in his rear-view mirror, before pulling out to overtake a truck.

"Okay, dumb question. Why isn't it mandatory?" Liz asked.

"Function of government. Never enough money to go around. Being the coroner of a city as large as San Francisco with an active criminal population makes for judgment decisions, like which deaths should be autopsied, and which shouldn't. Quite frankly, there isn't enough money or manpower to do all of them. An elderly person with no visible signs of trauma would be a natural to take a pass on, and in this case, that's unfortunate because it's causing problems."

"Roger, from that statement, I'm taking it you think Bernie Spitzer was murdered. Right?"

He was quiet for several moments, and then he said, "Liz, if it was the old guy down the street who tended his roses, and he died with no signs of trauma, no one would blink twice. Matter of fact, rather doubt that anyone would request that an autopsy be conducted, but that wasn't the case here.

"The man died with no will or trust, which in itself is unusual, then he has two children who have both had monetary problems, a much younger woman as a companion, and a business deal from the past that went bad. Yeah, I sure would have liked to have seen an autopsy conducted immediately upon his death. Cases go stale, suspects have time to develop elaborate alibis, and evidence gets inadvertently or deliberately lost. In cases like that, when I'm called in to defend someone, it makes my job a lot harder."

Liz thought for a moment. "I can see where it would. I'll call Sean first thing tomorrow and start doing what I can to help, although I have no idea what it would be. What did you think about the news that Michelle's expecting twins?"

"I'm kind of at odds over that." Roger looked across at Liz for a brief second and she could see that like her, he was tired too. He turned his attention back to the road. "Naturally, if she's happy I'm happy for her, but if Bernie was murdered, his son and daughter have got to be placed very high on the suspect list. Couple that with the fact that not only is Walter going to court to ask for an increase in Michelle's family allowance, which will take money from the estate, but also the share each of them will inherit will go down from one-third to one-fourth now that Michelle's going to have twins rather than just one child. When you're dealing with an estate as large as Bernie's looks to be, that's a sizable chunk of money. If you do the math, it reduces each of their shares from $100 hundred million, with one child, to $75 million, with the twins. That's a $25 million decrease, and like I said, that's a sizeable chunk of money." He tapped his fingers on the steering wheel.

"Yes, I see what you mean. So, let me get this straight. When the twins are born, they and his adult children will split the estate equally, is that correct?" Liz asked him.

"Yes, and there's another thing we need to consider. I've been thinking about it the last couple of hours. Here it is. I think Michelle needs a bodyguard."

Liz looked at him, surprised. "A bodyguard? Why?"

"Liz, I know you like to believe the best will always come out in people, but if something horrible were to happen to Michelle and she had a miscarriage, or I guess in this case, it would be called two miscarriages, Bernie's adult son and daughter would each get one-half of his estate, not one-fourth."

Liz's eyes became wide with the realization of what he was saying. "Oh, Roger, you don't think they would try to do something to Michelle, do you?"

"I don't know, but I'd like to make sure my client is protected. I'll call Walter in the morning, and tell him what I have in mind. I've used several bodyguards in the past, so I can easily get one or two for her. Actually, I'll probably need two, because I'd like to see her guarded 24/7 until this whole thing shakes out."

"How do you think she'll feel about having bodyguards? I sure wouldn't like it." Michelle struck Liz as someone who didn't like to draw much attention to herself, despite her head-turning appearance.

"I have no idea, but considering what the consequences could be if she doesn't, her thoughts on the matter are rather irrelevant to me. I'll ask Walter to call her and tell her it's a done deal. I think I'll also have a talk with the doorman or doormen, since there are probably several, grease their palms, and tell them I'd like them to keep a log of anyone who asks for Ms. D'Amato, and to call me if anyone asks about her condo number. I also want them to hold any flowers or packages in the lobby until I can have her bodyguards inspect them.

"I noticed that a key was needed for the regular elevator as well as Bernie's, so that should help keep foot traffic to her condo down." He paused, looked at Liz, and resumed speaking. "Liz, I know you don't like to hear this, but until we find out exactly what's happening here, I'd like Winston to be with you at all times." He saw her start to object and held his hand up to stop her from speaking.

"It's not up for negotiation," he insisted. "I need to spend time doing whatever it takes to make sure that in case Michelle is considered to be a suspect, or worst-case scenario, is charged with murder, she gets the best representation money can buy. Walter needs to get his case ready to ask for the increased family allowance for her and the babies, and remember that's going to be on a fast track, plus he has to keep her as calm as reasonably possible. And you, my love, will be the one out among them, trying to see what you can find out about the cast of characters on the suspect list. That's why I want Winston with you, and if you really love me, you'd stick that little gun you own in your purse and have it with you all the time."

"Okay, Roger," Liz said, knowing there was no point arguing with her husband. "I'll take Winston with me when I go into San Francisco, and since all the players live there, I'll probably be spending some time there, but seriously, the gun? You know how much I hate to have it on me. I always feel like a criminal myself when I'm carrying it."

"Sorry, Liz, but you have two choices. You can carry it and feel like a criminal or not carry it, and when something horrible happens, wish you'd had it. Personally, I'd opt for the former."

She sighed and said, "All right, if it makes you happy I will, but I have to tell you the only reason I'll do it is for your peace of mind. Turning to another matter, what did you think of the vibes between Michelle and Walter?"

"I have no clue what you're talking about. Walter is her attorney. And if you're referring to the fact he had his secretary get a sandwich and milk for her, of course he's going to try and do what he thinks is best for her and for her babies to be."

"Roger, are you telling me you didn't notice any chemistry between them?" she asked incredulously.

He took his eyes from the road ahead of him and looked briefly at her. His expression was clueless. "No, I didn't see any chemistry, and for what it's worth, I didn't see any physics either. I saw nothing more than a concerned attorney doing the best job he could for his client."

Liz started to giggle. "Roger, I love you more than anything, but I think you were absent when they handed out the man-woman vibe gene."

CHAPTER SEVENTEEN

"Are you going into your office in San Francisco today, or will you be working out of your office here in Red Cedar?" Liz asked Roger over breakfast the following morning. As usual, Winston was lying down contentedly between them. Although Liz was his go-to person, he'd accepted Roger as his second person when Liz and Roger had gotten married.

Before he married Liz, Roger had been a widower for several years. He'd lived and worked in San Francisco, but when he'd met Liz, his life had changed. He'd convinced his partners at the San Francisco law firm where he was a partner, that he should open a satellite office in Red Cedar. When he'd married, Liz, he acquired two grown step-children, as well as two dogs, Winston and Brandy Boy. It had been an interesting two years for Roger.

"Yes, I'm going to go into the city as soon as I finish breakfast. I want to get started doing the preliminary work on Michelle's case. Hate to say it, but I have a sense it's going to be needed. I want to look at all of the files we have on Bernie, I want to get the bodyguards for Michelle, and I want to talk to Sean. And you?" Roger asked as he looked up from buttering his toast.

"I'm calling Sean as soon as the office opens. You'll probably still be in transit, but he's so good at finding out information, I'd like him to get started on it as soon as possible. How about if I ask him to copy you on everything he finds out? That would save you from spending time telling him pretty much the same thing I'll be telling him."

"Please do," Roger responded with an affirmative nod of his head. "This is an interesting situation, Liz, with quite a cast of interesting characters. Although we still don't know if Bernie was murdered, but if he was, it's important to remember that there's always the chance it was committed by someone that's not even on our radar."

"I know, but I think it was my favorite defense attorney who once told me that when you're trying to solve a case you always start with the low hanging fruit, and based on what Sean finds out, that's what I'll be doing. Do you think you'll be back in your Red Cedar office later this afternoon? I was wondering if you'd be around for the guest dinner tonight."

"Probably not." Roger stuffed the last piece of toast in his mouth, and chewed it before replying. "I want to see where this goes. There's a good chance that Bernie's children will have their attorney get a court order to exhume the body, and if that happens, we could know something pretty soon. Sounds like Walter has a source at the police department, so I want to make sure I'm told as soon as he finds out anything. And you?"

Liz stirred her morning drink of choice, a concoction of warm water, lemon, and manuka honey. "I mentioned the guest dinner, but depending on what Sean finds out, I may go into the city and if that happens, I won't be able to make it back here in time for dinner. I hate to do that to Gina two nights in a row, but I think Michelle's predicament takes precedence."

"Couldn't agree more." Roger looked down at the watch on his wrist and took a final sip of his coffee. "I need to get out of here. The longer I wait, the worse the traffic will be. If I leave now, I might be able to beat the bulk of it. I'm so glad the firm agreed to let me open an office here in Red Cedar. I don't even want to think what my stress level and blood pressure would be like if I had to make that commute on a daily basis."

Roger stood up, walked around the table, and kissed Liz on her cheek. "Love you, Mrs. Langley. I'll touch base with you later today. If you're going to be in the city, maybe we could have lunch or an early dinner there." Winston followed him to the door and watched him step over Brandy Boy to get to the steps that led down to where his car was parked.

"Okay, Winston. It's just you and me," Liz said to the big dog after Roger had left. "You haven't been to the city in a while. This might be the day."

She looked at the kitchen clock, and although it was only 7:00, she knew Sean often went into the office early to make up for the times he left the office in the afternoon to coach his nephew's soccer team. Sean had two loves in life: his work and the soccer team. He was still searching for a woman who could become his third love, or maybe even his first, but so far, he was scoreless in that department.

She reached for her phone and pressed in Sean's number, smiling when he picked it up. "Morning, Sean. I took a chance and thought I'd see if you were at the office this early. Guess I made the right decision."

"You did. I'm leaving the office early today. My team has a big game, so I thought I'd come in and take care of the daily grind. Liz, whenever you call this early, I'm guessing this is not just to say hi and see how I'm doing. Would that be correct?"

Liz laughed. "That it would. A situation has come up that needs your expertise. Let me give you the background and the names of the players. I'd like any information you can find out about these people." She spent the next few minutes telling him about Michelle's situation and the list of possible suspects.

"When do you need this, Liz? I'm actually pretty open this morning. I have a meeting at 1:00 with one of the partners regarding a high-profile divorce. Seems like the husband might have been supporting not one, but apparently two mistresses. He can well afford it, but the wife wants to use whatever I can find out to help her get the best settlement she can. At least that's what her family law attorney told me."

"Sean, I hate to ask, but Roger may not have the luxury of a long time to prepare the defense in this case, if it comes to that. Considering the stress Michelle is under, and don't forget, I mentioned she was carrying twins, I'd like to get started on this as soon as possible, and I know Roger would too. By the way, to save both you and Roger time, in addition to telling me whatever you find out, would you make sure that he gets the information as well?"

"Sure, that's not a problem. It's only a little after 7:00 right now, so I can probably have something for you by 10:00. Is that soon enough?"

"That would be wonderful, and it will give me a chance to get tonight's dinner organized for Gina in case I have to go into the city."

"Well, if you do, you know you're always welcome to come to one of our soccer games. This evening we're practicing for tomorrow's game. That's for the league championship, and I can't even begin to tell you how excited this team of twelve-year-old boys is."

"Sounds to me like the coach is, too."

"You've got that right," Sean said. "Talk to you later."

CHAPTER EIGHTEEN

Liz spent the next two hours preparing and assembling that night's dinner in case she had to go to San Francisco. She wrote out instructions for Gina and thought how very lucky she was to have someone who could handle the dinners when she couldn't be there to do them herself.

Winston may have been an excellent guard dog, highly trained to voice and hand signal commands, and a gentle giant, but he was still a dog. And this dog did what most dogs do when their owner is opening up the refrigerator and working in the kitchen. He simply stayed as close to her as he could, hoping that an errant crumb would find its way to the floor, and he would be the one to discover it. It was a game he and Liz played almost every day, and both of them knew the rules well.

True to the game, Liz "accidentally" allowed several choice morsels to fall to the floor. And if a stranger were to witness the game, they might be amazed that the morsels that fell to the floor were always of interest to Winston, not something mundane like celery or brussel sprouts. "Okay, Winston, the game is over for today." Liz washed her hands quickly with warm water and soap. "My phone's ringing, and I can see from the name on the screen that it's Sean."

"Sean, you're true to your word. It's 10:00 straight up. I assume you have some information for me."

"No, Liz, not some information. I have a lot of information for you. Where do you want me to start?"

Liz sat down at the kitchen table. "How about with Michelle? She's kind of the main player here."

"Okay, your call. She was bounced around between a number of different foster homes when she was growing up, and although I didn't find any information alluding to foster fathers overstepping boundaries with her, the fact that she left the last one when she was only sixteen sure could be a factor. From what I found out, she was a beautiful young woman, and from recent photos of her with Bernie, she is still drop-dead gorgeous nearly twenty-five years later."

"Yes, I'd agree. She is a stunningly beautiful woman," Liz said.

"According to my research, a modeling agency picked her up, and she spent a couple of years working for them in Europe. Some of the countries there aren't quite as restrictive as the U.S. is about underage girls working. She quit modeling when she got married for the first time. Husband number one was a Brazilian soccer player, and although he was quite well known for his exploits on the soccer field, he was equally at home in the beds of a number of other women. He spent money lavishly, to the extent that when Michelle divorced him, she left the marriage with very little."

"I see," Liz said, glad to see that Michelle hadn't been accepting of her husband's philandering. "What happened with husband number two?"

"Her second husband was the heir apparent to become the president of one of the top perfume companies in France, or at least that's what he told her. What he didn't tell her was the company was about to be bought out by an American company, and he was no longer the heir. In fact, once the acquisition was complete, he was out of a job. Evidently he decided to take a proactive approach and rather than slink away into the sunset, he announced his intention to join a Buddhist monastery in Thailand. Their divorce soon followed."

"Wow! What a background. I knew nothing about either the first marriage or that one. Go on. Shock me with husband number three."

"Michelle discovered him when she was working as a bank teller. She desperately needed a job, since she was getting a little long in the tooth for modeling, and the manager of a bank on Wall Street was more than happy to hire her, although I don't think it was for her banking experience, because she didn't have any. Anyway, she met number three when he was making a bank deposit. Within a few weeks, she'd left the bank and become his wife. He was quite wealthy, but he'd omitted one little fact which cost him two marriages. He liked to play around with the hired help. She left that marriage with some money, but once again Michelle was divorced."

"What a life that woman has lived and now this." Liz admired Michelle for being so strong and a survivor, in spite of all she'd been through. "Did you find out how she met Bernie? She told me, but I can't remember."

"According to an article I read she met him at some event when she was still married to number three. I read in some rag that he'd given her his business card and said if she was ever free to do so, he'd love to have dinner with her. Guess guys as rich as Bernie Spitzer don't mind poaching. Anyway, from what the article said, she called him after she was divorced, and they became a couple from then on. I also read where she literally bumped into him at a law office. Anyway, he bought her a condominium in the same building as his, an expensive car, fancy jewelry, and gave her a very large monthly allowance, although he was adamant about not ever getting married again."

"I remember. It was the second one. Now I understand even more why having children is so important to Michelle. Seems like she's never had anything remotely resembling a stable life. Glamourous, yes, normal no. Let me ask you one other question, and since you didn't bring anything up about it, I'm assuming the answer is no. Did you find out anything negative about her, such as arrests, drug use, alcohol use, things of that nature?"

"No, I never even saw a hint that she was anything less than a person who had been victimized by a number of events over which she had no control. Have to tell you after doing the research on her, I'm on her side. The lady deserves a break."

"She has no history of being involved in anything that seems to be the least bit illegal or even in any gray areas, right?"

"Right, why are you asking?"

"Sean, did you find anything that would point to her knowing that if she conceived Bernie's children after his death by means of artificial insemination and then had them after his death, that they would be heirs to his fortune?"

"Not a thing, but I'm not sure information like that would be readily accessible. Do you know who told her that a new law in California had been enacted concerning that type of situation?"

"I think it was her attorney. It was my understanding based on a lunch I had with her shortly after we met, that she simply wanted to have Bernie's child. I was under the impression it had nothing to do with his estate."

"Liz, the doctor who oversaw the artificial insemination might have been aware of it. Maybe he was the one who told her. Do you have his name?"

"No, I'll follow up on that. It might be relevant. Sean, can I get right back to you? Winston is standing at the door with an urgent look on his face. It will be just a few minutes."

"I'll be here. Talk to you in a few."

CHAPTER NINETEEN

"Sorry, Sean," Liz said a few minutes later when she called him back. "Winston needed to go outside and the look on his face told me I couldn't put it off. Maybe I dropped too many crumbs on the floor for him."

"Hate to say anything, Liz, but I think that dog has a better life than most of the people living in the United States. When I come back, I want to come back as a Langley dog."

"You're probably right, Sean, but he sure has been there a couple of times when I needed some help. A snack here and there is a small price to pay for him saving my life."

"Okay, I grant you that one. Back to the list of suspects. I looked into Jim Brown, and I thought it was kind of a sad case. I try not to make moral judgments on people after I conduct a background investigation, but I wonder if Bernie Spitzer's appetite for money and success kind of got away from him here."

"What do you mean?" Liz asked.

"Well, I'm not getting paid to say someone did something right or wrong, but I'm having a hard time with this one. Seems like Bernie kind of pulled a fast one on Brown when he got an important patent registered in his name alone and left Brown hanging out to dry. Sure, it could have been an honest mistake, but all Bernie had to do was say that he'd register the patent in both of their names, but he didn't. He registered it only in his name, forced Brown out of the company they both had formed, paid him a paltry sum for all of Brown's work, and then he owns this fabulous money machine company free and clear. Not to mention the fact that he sold it for a bundle a few years later. Kind of smells in my book."

"I rather imagine that's what Brown thought, too, judging from the note I told you about. Did you find out anything about what Brown did after he left the company?"

"Pretty much what you told me. Brown never did much with his life after that. He bounced around in a couple of jobs, but guess his heart wasn't in it. His wife left him, he lost his house, and for the rest of his life he's pretty much been circling the drain. He's living, or should I say, existing, on Social Security. He's been diagnosed with pancreatic cancer, and from what I was able to find out, the outlook is not too rosy. Like I said, I feel sorry for the guy."

"Sorry or not, the bottom line is did he hate what Bernie Spitzer did to him enough to kill him? That's the question," Liz said. "Plus, what immediately comes to my mind is how would someone that down on their luck get past the doorman in a swanky condominium?"

"That, Madam Sleuth, I don't know. Guess that's why you're paid the big bucks."

"Right, Sean. Good thing I have a lawyer for a husband and a successful spa business, or my pro bono work would have to end. What else did you find out?"

"This case, if it turns out to be a case, has some pretty undesirable characters in it. Bernie's daughter, Joni Toscano, is married to Rocco Toscano. He's bad through and through. He's worked for the Luchese crime family since he was in his teens. Word has it that the only reason he married Joni was to get his hands on her dad's money. He's a two-bit criminal, but he sure would have the resources to have his father-in-law murdered. I found out he just spent the little money he and Joni have to get in on a piece of the action for some new business deal he thinks will make him rich. Looks like he promised he could get his hands on a lot more money very soon, and that what he'd paid to get into the deal was just a down payment."

"Are you thinking he killed Bernie, so Joni would get her inheritance?"

"I'm not being paid to interpret the facts, Liz, that's what you and Roger do. I do find it interesting that a man who has a violent temper and has been arrested a number of time for violent crimes including assault and battery, has entered into a shady business agreement, has told his future business partners that what he paid was just the down payment, and the rest of the money will soon follow, then his father-in-law dies suddenly of natural causes, and he knows his wife is going to inherit one-half of his estate. At least he thought that was the case, until he found out that Michelle was carrying Bernie's baby, which now turns out to be two babies."

Liz shivered involuntarily. "Maybe I'm reading between the lines, but it seems to me you're suggesting that if Rocco was the one responsible for Bernie's murder, he wouldn't be thrilled with having to see his wife's share of the estate reduced because of the pending births."

"Like I said earlier, I'm just telling you the facts, but yes, I think that's a fair analysis."

"Sean, you said Rocco had been arrested for assault and battery. Was he ever convicted or did he do time for them?"

"No, he was lawyered up immediately by the attorney for the Luchese family. Guy's dirty, but he has a heck of an attorney, and that attorney got him off every time. The police were called to the family home several times by Joni for domestic abuse, but each time she refused to file charges against Rocco, and the charges were dropped."

"He sounds like a real sweetheart," Liz said, making some notes on a pad of paper. "No wonder Roger thought Michelle should have a bodyguard 24/7. At the time, I thought he was overreacting, but given all this information, I think he was absolutely right. That leaves Bernie's son, Larry Spitzer. What did you find out about him?"

"He's a loser, a real loser," Sean said. "I went back a lot of years and found out he was kicked out of college for cheating on an exam and when the cheat sheet was found on him, so was a stash of cocaine."

"That seems like a pretty dumb thing to do."

"It was, but no one ever said Larry Spitzer was going to give Albert Einstein a run for his money. Since that time his life has consisted of a series of drug rehabs and get-rich-schemes that never made enough money to even pay him back the entry fee. Talk has it that Bernie was getting ready to disinherit him."

"So, reading between the lines, if Bernie dies before he formally disinherits Larry, that means Larry inherits half of Bernie's estate as one of Bernie's two heirs-at-law, is that right?" Liz said. "The other heir being his sister, Joni. Of course, the shares they will now receive are going to be reduced by half because of the impending birth of twins. That could be a pretty powerful motive for someone who was looking at no other options."

"Yes, that it could." Sean sounded distracted, and Liz could hear voices in the background. "Liz, I need to take care of a few things here at the office. If you find out something else, give me a call, and I'll make sure Roger has all this information. I've sent you some pictures of the players, so if you run across any of them, you'll recognize them. One last thing, here's the contact information for everyone. Knowing you, you're probably going to want to talk to them or at least their neighbors." Liz wrote down the addresses and phone numbers he related to her.

"As always, Sean, thanks. At least you'll get paid for providing me with this information. Bill Roger since he's working on the defense angle."

"Will do."

"One last thing, Sean. Good luck with the game tomorrow night."

"The boys and I thank you."

CHAPTER TWENTY

Liz looked over the notes she'd written out for Gina to make sure they'd be easy for her to interpret and apologized for having to be gone two nights in a row. Although she really didn't like to be away from the spa during the guest dinners, she felt that Michelle's problem trumped her role of being the congenial hostess.

She spent the next hour researching the suspects' addresses on the Internet, printed out maps and directions, changed clothes, and took Winston outside to commune with nature before she put him in her van for the hour long drive into San Francisco.

"Winston, it looks like we need go into the city. Roger made me promise I'd take you, so like it or not, you're stuck with me for the next few hours."

The big dog wagged his tail as she spoke to him, and she was certain that he understood every word she was saying. As ridiculous as it felt, she and Roger had resorted to spelling certain words such as "ride," because he understood perfectly well what that word meant and would always run to the door as soon as either one of them said it. She didn't think San Francisco was in his word repertoire, but she imagined it would be after today.

Traffic was relatively light, and she felt her heart beat a little faster the closer she got to the city. She loved Red Cedar, and never regretted moving to the slower paced small rural town, but there was just something magical about San Francisco. Although she hadn't left her heart there, as the famous Tony Bennett song said, the thought of the distinctive nature of the city never failed to thrill her.

She loved it all – the cable cars, North Beach with it's wonderful Italian stores and restaurants, the fog, the steep rolling hills, the eclectic mix of architectural styles from the Victorian "painted lady" homes to the Coit Tower and the Palace of Fine Arts. She loved it when the fog cleared enough that she could see the Golden Gate bridge and the island where the former Alcatraz Federal Penitentiary had been located.

Liz smiled remembering the many times she'd taken her children, Jonah and Brittany, to Chinatown and Fisherman's Wharf. Brittany was always mesmerized by the street mimes. *Yes,* Liz thought, *there's an energy in the city like nowhere else I've ever been, and I love it, but it is nice to be able to return to the peace and quiet of Red Cedar.*

She easily drove to a run-down neighborhood that had seen better days. The apartment where Jim Brown lived was housed in a boxy, brown building. It had been built in an architectural time when everything was uniform, from the measured distance between the windows to the equal number of apartments on the left and the right. Liz imagined that the apartments inside the building were all exactly the same, except for what the tenants had done to them over the years.

Liz wasn't sure what the response from the tenants would be if a large boxer entered their building, and since it was early afternoon, she didn't think she'd be in any danger. "I'll be back in a few minutes, Winston. You guard the van."

She got out of her van and closed the door. Immediately Winston jumped up and put his front paws on the console between the passenger and driver's seat, looking from one side to another. Obviously, he had taken her command literally. She knew that her van would be very safe in her absence, actually, probably safer than if she'd been in it.

As she walked up to the front door of the aging apartment building, she noticed the weeds that had grown up in the cracks in the cement walk and the paint chipping off of the door. She easily opened the door and walked over to where the elevator was located. There was a tenant roster next to it and she saw the name Jim Brown on it and his apartment number, 3B. She stepped into the elevator and was immediately overcome with the smell of stale smoke and urine. She wondered if the homeless used it to sleep in at night. It was all she could do to keep from retching.

When the door opened on the third floor, she quickly got out, but realized she was only exchanging the smells from the elevator for those of rancid oils and the sweet smell of marijuana. It looked like the frayed dirty brown carpeting in the hall hadn't been vacuumed, much less cleaned, in a long, long time. Liz walked down the hall to 3B, took a deep breath, and rang the doorbell button which was hanging from a wire attached to the doorbell. There was no answer.

She listened, but didn't hear any sounds coming from inside the apartment, so she tried knocking. Again, there was no answer. About that time a man and a woman opened the door at the end of the hallway which led up from the stairway. They walked down the hall towards Liz and stopped at the apartment next to Jim Brown's.

The woman was putting her key in the door while the man lit a cigarette. "Excuse me," Liz said, turning to face them. "Is this the apartment where Jim Brown lives? No one's answering, and I want to make sure I have the right one."

The man looked at her and she realized it was the doorman she'd seen at Michelle's condominium building the evening before. "Aren't you Joe, the doorman at the condominium where Michelle D'Amato lives?" she asked.

"Yes, why do you ask?" he said. Even though the door to their apartment was now open, the woman with him was standing in the doorway, listening to their conversation.

"I recognized you from when Michelle said hello to you last night.

She's a friend of mine."

"You got good friends. She's a nice lady. Shame about Mr. Spitzer. I've known him a long time, but guess when you're that old, your time has come."

What an insensitive thing to say, Liz thought. *For all he knows I could be related to Bernie.*

"You asked about Jim. Yeah, that's his place, but he's not usually at home most days."

"Well, that explains why he didn't answer the doorbell or my knock. You said most days. Does he go somewhere special every day?" Liz asked, thinking if Sean's information was right, he might be going to a doctor for chemotherapy or radiation treatments.

"Well, it's not that special, but he loves to go to the park that's two blocks down the street. He says he reads the paper and thinks about what his life would have been if it had turned out otherwise. Poor guy. From what he's told me, he caught some bad breaks."

"I'm sorry. I don't know what you mean."

"Let's just say Bernie Spitzer did him dirty. If it sounded like I wasn't too sorry that Bernie died, there's some truth to that. I'm sorry for Miss Michelle, because I like her. She always treats me right, you know, remembers my name and all. Even gives me an envelope with money in it each Christmas. Spitzer never did that. Don't think too many people shed tears over his death, except for all them organizations he donated to. Sure never saw that he had a family that cared enough to come around, and can't say I'm surprised. Never know what Miss Michelle saw in him."

"I never met him, so I know nothing about him. Where did you say the park was located? I'd like to talk to Mr. Brown."

"Go down the street two blocks," he said gesturing in the direction of the park, "and turn left. It's right there. Back in the day of clean open spaces it was pretty nice, but at least there's a little green left among all these buildings. Nice talking to you, but I've got to go. I need to change clothes. My shift starts in a little while."

Interesting, Liz thought, as she headed down the stairs in lieu of taking the elevator. *If it's determined that Bernie was murdered, and one of the suspects is Jim Brown, sure is convenient he knows the doorman at the condominium building where Bernie lived. It wouldn't be much of a stretch to think the doorman might have given Jim access to Bernie's condominium. That's quite a coincidence, and I don't like coincidences when I'm investigating a murder.*

CHAPTER TWENTY-ONE

Liz walked back to her van, opened the door, and said, "Winston, I think it's time for a walk, and from what I hear, there's a little park not too far away. You can get some exercise, and I'll make Roger happy by taking you with me. Ready?"

Winston clearly understood the word "ready" and jumped down onto the sidewalk while Liz secured his leash to his collar. It wasn't that she felt it was necessary, but the last thing she wanted to do was get a citation for having a dog off leash.

She easily found the park and walked through it, avoiding the mothers jogging with baby strollers in front of them while they were talking on their cell phones, the people who were walking their dogs and felt that the leash laws didn't apply to them and their dogs, as well as the homeless people, some of whom she saw panhandling. While it would never compete with a park in an upscale neighborhood, she had to admit there was some charm to it. The city or someone had planted flowers and litter had been kept to a minimum. She wondered if there was a neighborhood group that had made keeping the park clean their cause, but in a neighborhood as rundown as this one, that would be rare.

There were several park benches with people sitting on them. Her attention was drawn to a stoop-shouldered, bespectacled elderly man who wore a moth-eaten grey cardigan sweater, even though the day was warm, and was reading a newspaper. He looked a lot like the man in the photograph Sean had sent her.

Liz stood nearby, talking to Winston, as she tried to decide what would be the best way to approach the man. She couldn't help but feel sorry for him, thinking about how he'd been forced out of a lucrative company he'd helped build, and in his twilight years, getting cancer. Just then she noticed a piece of paper on the ground.

"Excuse me, sir, is this paper yours?" she asked.

The man looked up from his newspaper and took the paper she handed him. He looked at it and said, "No, actually it looks like a grocery list, and I sure don't have the kind of money the food on this list would cost. Someone must have dropped it." He looked over at Winston. "Nice looking dog you've got there."

"Thanks, that's the reason I'm here. He came into town with me today, and I thought he might like a walk in the park after the drive in. It's quite a nice little park. Do you come here often?" she asked.

"Sure do. I live in a little apartment not far from here that gives me claustrophobia if I stay in it too long, so I'm here most days. Somebody leaves a paper here every day at about lunchtime, and if I time it right, I can pick up the paper and read what's going on here in San Francisco and everywhere else in the world."

"It probably goes well with that cup of coffee you've got."

"That it does. Can't afford to buy a cup anymore, so I make one before I come here. Works out just fine. I've learned how to adjust over the years," he said without a trace of rancor. "Here, have a seat. Plenty of room on the bench for one more."

Liz accepted his offer and sat down on the bench beside him. "When you say you've learned how to adjust, I take it that your circumstances have changed," she said softly.

"You can say that again. You might not know it by looking at me now, but once I was the part-owner of a company that later was sold for millions. Course I wasn't an owner when it was sold."

"That sounds like a sad story," Liz said.

"Probably depends on who you're talking to. From my point of view, it's a very sad story. I made a mistake and it cost me my job, my wife, my home and put me where I am now. Plus, now I've got the big C. I'm not sure how it could get any sadder." He laughed bitterly. "Maybe I should sell my life story to some big movie studio, and they'd get all the money from it, just like my former partner did, and I'd come out with almost nothing. Maybe that's just the way my life is."

"My name's Liz Langley, sir, and you've aroused my curiosity. What was your mistake, if I might ask?"

He put his hand out and shook hers. "Name's Jim Brown. I was a co-founder of a company that made a specialized part for a scientific product, it's pretty technical and unimportant, but I developed it, and I know it sounds stupid, but I never got around to getting a patent for it. If I had, I can tell you my life would be a lot different than it is now."

"What happened?" she asked.

"My partner found out we were selling the product with no patent protection. He went ballistic, and decided to get the patent in his own name. When he told me he'd done that, I didn't have any proof that I was the one who had actually come up with the design for the product. When he offered me money to sign the company over to him, or he'd simply view me as an employee, and pay me accordingly, I really didn't have a choice. In his eyes, I was no longer his partner, and I sure didn't have anything that would lead a judge to believe I was entitled to half the company's assets."

"What did you do?" Liz asked, although she already knew the answer.

"I did the only thing I thought I could do, and in retrospect, I still think it was the right decision. I took the money and ran. Unfortunately, my wife didn't see it that way. She called me stupid when she walked out of the door for the last time. Maybe she was right."

"How so?"

"I lost the money Bernie Spitzer had paid me for the company in a poker game. I wound up with almost no money, and I couldn't make my house payments. We'd bought a nice home in Lafayette, but that went, along with everything else. By then the word on the street was that I'd really screwed up, so no one in the industry would hire me. I was a little too old to get a job slinging fast food, so I survived until I got on Social Security, and here I am."

"That is sad, Mr. Brown. I imagine you must really resent Bernie Spitzer."

"Liz, if I might call you that, the answer to that question used to be an automatic yes, but lately I've kind of changed. You see, in addition to everything else, like I said, I have cancer, and from what the doctors tell me, it's incurable. That's definitely shaped my thinking. I wonder if I got it because I spent so much of my life hating someone. Maybe hatred and cancer are the same thing. They eat at you from inside." Jim's eyes were almost lifeless, like the lights had already gone out.

"That's quite an interesting thought." Liz looked at the children playing on the grass, thinking how soul-destroying it must be to wake up one day with not much time left, regretting how you'd spent your life.

"Yeah, I'm getting to be a real philosopher in my old age," Jim said, rolling his eyes. "I saw in the paper a few months ago where Bernie had died. They said it was because of old age, and it may have been. I used to spend a lot of time and energy thinking how great it would be if he died. Matter of fact, even ran a couple of scenarios through my mind about how I might help make that happen, but after I was diagnosed, those thoughts went away." He pulled his thin sweater tighter around his frail frame.

"I need every ounce of strength and positive thinking that I have left, not negative thinking, to see if I can at least bring this monster that's in me to remission, even if I can't make it go away. So, compared to what I would have thought about his death years and even months ago, all I felt when I saw the article was a profound sadness at wasting my life with so much hatred eating away at me. Believe me, I wish I could get back all that strength and energy I wasted for so many years."

Liz leaned closer to him and patted his arm. He didn't pull away, and they sat like that for a while. "Thanks for talking to me, Jim. I'm so sorry. Is there anything I, as a stranger, can do?"

"Yeah, you can let me pet that dog, if he'll let me. Had one that didn't look too different from him years ago, but even if the place I live allowed dogs, I couldn't afford to feed the thing."

"Winston, it's okay," Liz said as Jim reached his hand down to let Winston sniff him. After a moment Liz and Jim were quiet while he petted Winston who stepped closer and rested his head on Jim's leg. Liz took a deep breath, willing the tears that threatened to gather in her eyes, to stay in place until she could get back to her van.

CHAPTER TWENTY-TWO

After her meeting with Jim Brown, Liz and Winston walked back to her van, but she couldn't shake the sad feeling she had about the way Jim's life had turned out. She kept thinking how different it would have been if he'd just filed the necessary paperwork for the patent. That was certainly the start of his downhill spiral that wound up leaving him with nothing. She had just adjusted her seat belt when her phone rang. It was Roger.

"Hi, sweetheart," he said. "How's your day coming along, and where are you?"

"I'm in San Francisco, and I wish I could tell you that my day was just terrific, but I'd be lying. I just met with Jim Brown, and after listening to his sad story, there's no way he should be on the suspect list if it's determined that Bernie was murdered."

"I wish I could tell you that your day was going to get better, but I don't think I can. I want to hear all about your meeting with Jim, but I have a little emergency on my hands, and one you should be aware of before you blindly go off and talk to people."

"What are you talking about, Roger? What's happened?"

"I don't think there's any way to sugarcoat this, so here goes. I just got a call from Walter, and his source at the police department, Mitch

Latham, called him and told him that Bernie's two children were able to get an emergency court order to have Bernie's body exhumed. There is a provision in the law that if a judge signs an authorization order, an autopsy can be conducted almost immediately, and that's exactly what happened. Unfortunately, Bernie did not die of natural causes. The autopsy clearly showed that he was poisoned. Naturally, that puts Michelle in a very bad light, and in some ways, puts his children in a good light."

"Oh no!"

"If it goes to trial, and keep in mind I have to think of all the things that could happen, the prosecuting attorney will probably make a big deal about the fact that it was his children who asked for the body to be exhumed and an autopsy conducted. I'm not saying one of them or both of them aren't involved in Bernie's murder, but since they were the ones who asked for the autopsy, it would be a hard thing to refute. Plus, I have to think a jury or a judge would automatically think they wouldn't ask for an autopsy if they were guilty. A lot of jurors would never make the leap that maybe they did that in order to take the spotlight away from themselves, but I'll deal with that if and when I have to. Anyway, Walter has requested a meeting this afternoon with Michelle and me. Since you're in town, you might want to be there."

"I very much would, and I can tell all of you about Jim Brown then. What time?"

"Five in Walter's office. Liz, I know you told me you'd carry your gun and keep Winston with you, but since we're now dealing with a murder case, I want to make sure you're doing that."

Liz looked over her shoulder to where an alert Winston was panting in her ear. "Winston's sitting in the back seat of my van as we speak. As a matter of fact, I even took him to the park when I talked to Jim Brown, and I have my gun in my purse. That should make you happy," Liz said.

"I'm not sure anyone else would understand why those two things make me happy, but let's say they do help to relieve my stress levels."

"Roger, have you talked to Michelle about this?"

"No. Walter had already talked to her when he called me, and he said she was quite shaken by the news."

"I don't blame her. Do you think I should call her or just wait until the meeting this afternoon?"

"Why don't you wait? She told Walter she was going to call her doctor and see if there was something she could take for her anxiety. She told him she doesn't want to take anything that might hurt the babies."

"That's something I know nothing about. Poor thing. Being pregnant with twins is enough of a stress without being a possible suspect in a murder case."

"I know. Liz, I'm sorry, but I need to spend the rest of the afternoon preparing a defense, or at least get my ducks in a row in case I have to. I'll see you at the meeting this afternoon. Loves."

Liz spent several minutes trying to decide what to do next. Now that Bernie's death was definitely confirmed as a murder, she knew that Michelle would probably be a prime suspect. In order to try and remove Michelle from the list of suspects, she decided to see what she could find out from Bernie's children. She checked the email she'd printed out from Sean, and realized she wasn't too far from where Bernie's son, Larry lived. She started her van and drove the short distance to where his apartment building was located.

When she arrived at the address Sean had sent, she felt like she was having a déjà vu experience. The apartment building where Larry lived looked like a clone of the one where Jim Brown lived. About the only difference between the two was that Larry's was a little larger. Like Jim's, weeds had grown up in the cracks in the cement walk and paint was flaking off of the front doors of the building.

She'd just pulled into a parking place a few doors down from the building when she saw the front door to the building open and a man stepped out. Liz quickly picked up the picture Sean had sent her. There was no doubt in her mind that the man walking down the steps was none other than Bernie's son, Larry Spitzer.

She debated whether to try and gain access to his apartment while he was gone in the hopes that she might find something useful or follow him. She decided it would be a lot safer for her if she observed him from a distance while other people were around rather than possibly getting caught in his apartment. She didn't know how she would be able to find a way into his apartment anyway, so following and watching him was her only viable option.

As she looked around, she decided she'd made the right decision. Several of the people walking down the sidewalk did not look like the type of people who would visit her spa or ones she'd meet at one of Roger's law office parties. They mostly looked like down-and-out individuals with a rough hardscrabble look about them.

Glad that she'd chosen to wear nondescript jeans and an old denim blouse, she took her watch and wedding ring off and put them in the glove compartment. When she and Winston stepped out of her van, she manually pushed the door lock rather than using the lock on her fob, not wanting the sound to draw attention to her.

She spotted Larry farther down the sidewalk and followed him for about two blocks. She watched as he walked into a neighborhood bar with a sign that said "Captain Kidd's" along with a large picture of a pirate displayed on it. As she walked by, she saw that the bar had an outdoor side patio. A moment later she noticed that Larry had taken a seat at a table on the patio. It was the type of bar that catered to the neighborhood locals, and she overheard several people call him Larry, which confirmed she was right in thinking the man in question was Larry Spitzer.

Liz turned around, walked in the front door, and over to the bar. "Excuse me," she said to the bartender, "I'm wondering if it would be all right if I take my dog to the patio area. I was walking by and thought a cold beer would taste good. Is that allowed?"

"For you, little lady, sure," he said winking, as the bar area became quiet with the arrival of a new attractive woman. "Matter of fact, a lot of folks bring their dogs here when they have an itch for a beer. It's right through that door. Course, from the looks of your dog, don't think anyone else will be taking their dog back there when they see that big brute."

She and Winston walked through the door and out to the small patio which had several tables with umbrellas over them, each bearing the name of a different brand of beer. She took a seat at an unoccupied table next to where Larry was sitting and noticed he was drinking a beer the barmaid had already brought him.

Hmmm, Liz thought, *he must be a regular if he already has his beer. The barmaid must have gotten it as soon as he walked in.*

The barmaid walked over to Liz and said, "What can I get ya', honey?"

Liz looked up at the woman who was about her age and the immediate saying of "rode hard and put away wet" came to mind. The skintight top, short black mini, and black band around her bleached blond hair with a feather sticking out of it, couldn't hide the fact that the years had not been kind to her. Her face was a roadmap of lines and even the black fishnet tights couldn't disguise the varicose veins which Liz thought must be causing her pain with all the standing and walking she must have to do in her job.

She looked over at where Larry was sitting and said, "Excuse me, sir. I haven't been here before. Can you recommend a good beer?"

"Sure, try the Anchor Steam Beer. That's what I always get. It's made in San Francisco, so I feel like I'm helping to support the local economy, right, Stella?" he said to the barmaid as they both laughed.

"I'll have one of those," Liz said. The barmaid left and a moment later Liz said, "There are so many beers on the market today, I get really confused. Thanks for helping me out."

"Not a problem. It's a lot easier when you just stick with one brand, leastways, that's what I do. Thing is, I only have a couple more months that I'll be drinking beer, because after that I'll be drinking the best champagne money can buy."

"Well, aren't you lucky? Have a big payday coming up?"

"You could say that. Got a lot of money coming my way. You ever hear of a man named Bernie Spitzer?" he asked.

Liz was quiet for a few minutes as if she was deep in thought. Just then the barmaid said, "Here ya' go. That'll be $4.50. It's happy hour time, so ya' got off light."

Larry interrupted. "Stella, put it on my tab. I'll take care of it." He moved over to the table where Liz was and sat down. She sensed that Winston wasn't thrilled with the idea and reached down to pet him and reassure him that it was all right.

"Nice dog you've got there," Larry said. "Pedigreed?"

"Yes. He was a gift to me. I don't think I could ever afford a pedigreed dog," she said.

"Well, I'm going to get one of those Argentine Mastiffs. Guess their Spanish name is *Dogo Argentino*. Hear they're the most expensive breed you can get. They're big suckers and great for protection. Want everyone to know that Larry Spitzer can afford the best."

Liz tightened her hold on Winston's leash, because Larry was sitting uncomfortably close to her and it made her nervous. "I thought I knew something about dogs, but that's a breed I've never heard of."

"Yeah, that doesn't surprise me. They're pretty rare. I'm thinking about six months from now I'll be sitting in some penthouse with my Argentinian Mastiff. Believe me, it's been a long dry spell for me, so

I'm looking forward to it. How do you like that beer?" Larry asked with a nod towards Liz's glass.

"It's quite good," Liz lied, not sharing that she hated beer. "You mentioned Bernie Spitzer. The name kind of rings a bell, but I can't place him."

Larry smiled, revealing stained teeth. "His name was in the papers all the time. He was my dad. He died a couple of months ago, but I just found out today he was murdered, and I'm pretty sure I know who did it."

"How sad. I'm so sorry. You say you think you know who did it?"

"I think so. Thing is, he had a young girlfriend who got herself knocked up after he died by using some of my old man's sperm he'd deposited in a sperm bank. Guess they passed some law a little while ago about how a woman could have a man's child after he died. Anyway, she's pregnant with his kid, actually it's not just one kid, she's carrying twins, and the thing is, looks like, according to the law, the kids she's carrying are going to be entitled to some of my old man's estate."

"I would think that would be a cause for being depressed about everything, not happy."

"No, see, here's the thing. I figure she'll be charged with his murder. I mean who else would have a motive like that? Sure, me and my sister are his only children, at least so far, but I figure once she's charged, the stress will cause her to miscarry. She's a little long in the tooth to be doing the new mommy thing. I mean she's at the far end of the spectrum."

Liz hoped her distaste for Larry wasn't apparent on her face. "I'm confused. How long has your father been dead?"

"About four months, but my sister and I figured his girlfriend would never get a red cent. Since he died without a will, my sister and I were his sole heirs, and we were in line to inherit everything. Then she went and got pregnant, and even petitioned the court for a family allowance, so that means her kid is going to get one-third of his estate. Then lo and behold, she finds out she's carrying twins. That reduced my take to one-fourth.

"My sister and I figure that's why she decided to have the kids, so she could get her hands on the money they're entitled to, but she got greedy. If she'd come to Joni and me, we might have given her something for all the years she was with dad, but not now. It's war, and with dad being murdered, I think there's a good chance she'll get charged with it. At least that's what our attorney is telling us."

Liz took a sip of her beer. The truth was that not only didn't she like beer, she had a hard time swallowing the bitter flavor of it. "I know nothing about legal things, but let me ask a dumb question. Since you and your sister are the heirs, why wouldn't either one of you be thought of as possible suspects?"

He looked around for Stella and motioned he'd like another beer. He glanced over at the beer Liz had in front of her and saw that it was still quite full. "Well, I got that covered. The night the old man died I was in a meeting with a bunch of men. Don't ask. I've had some bad experiences and my sponsor in the twelve-step program said I had to attend a meeting with him. Glad I did, because I've got a rock solid gold-plated alibi. Can't wait to see what her alibi will be."

"Wow," Liz said, her eyes widening. She was glad she'd followed Larry into the bar, because the more he drank, the more he talked, and that was exactly what she wanted him to do. "This sounds like something you'd see on television. What about your sister?"

"Joni was having a birthday party for her granddaughter, my great-niece. Her alibi is as solid as mine. Twenty parents will testify that she was at home with a bunch of snot-nosed kids running around. Nope, it was my dad's bimbo that did him in, and she's going to get hers. First of all, she'll have a miscarriage, then she'll go to prison, and then Joni and me will get it all, just the way it was before the bimbo came into the picture."

"I volunteered to have a birthday party for my granddaughter in a few weeks," Liz said with a light laugh. "Wish I could talk to your sister. It's been so long since I've had a child's birthday party, I have no idea what's done these days. Any chance you could give me her address and phone number, or would that be too presumptuous?" Liz asked, thinking that could be her entrée to his sister.

"Sure, she's a real homebody. Even cans her own apricots and peaches. She'd love to do that. I think she has a couple of pages on Etsy and Pinterest. She's really into crafts and baking. Here, I'll write it down for you."

He took a business card that had his name and phone number below the word "Entrepreneur." When he was finished he looked at his watch and said, "I've got to leave. Told my sponsor I'd meet him this afternoon for a meeting. He thinks he's helping me, and I like to humor him. Been nice talking to you," he said as he put a handful of breath mints in his mouth. He stood up, walked out of the patio, and back into the bar. A few moments later she saw him walking down the sidewalk, headed in the direction of his apartment.

Liz sat for a moment, stunned at what he was implying. It seemed like the exhuming of Bernie's body and the autopsy were more for the effect it would have on Michelle rather than anything having to do with trying to determine who murdered Bernie Spitzer. She almost felt sick as she stood, and with Winston on his leash, walked back to her van.

CHAPTER TWENTY-THREE

Although she already had Joni Toscano's address, the conversation with Larry had given her the perfect opening. She'd been struggling with how she could go about gaining access to Joni, and using the pretext of asking for information about how to have a successful child's birthday party was perfect. After she and Winston got in her car she called Joni.

The phone was answered on the first ring by a tentative female voice. "This is Joni."

"Hello, Joni. You don't know me. My name is Liz Lucas. I know this is going to sound kind of strange, but I was talking to your brother earlier today, and he mentioned that a few months ago you had a birthday party for your granddaughter. I told my daughter we could have my granddaughter's first birthday party at my home, but quite frankly, I don't have a clue how to host a birthday party these days. He gave me your address, and although I know I'm probably imposing, I happen to be in the neighborhood and wondered if I could stop by and talk to you for a few minutes. I promise I won't take up much of your time."

Liz had decided to use her former married name, Lucas, the name she'd gone by for so many years, rather than her current married name, on the off chance that Joni's attorney might have mentioned that Michelle's attorney was with a law firm who had a well-known defense attorney in it by the name of Roger Langley. She didn't want Joni to associate the name Langley with her.

Joni was quiet for several moments and then she said, "I agree it's a strange request, but I was lucky enough to have some help planning mine, so I guess I can repay the favor. I have to leave in about an hour, but if you could come now, that would be fine."

"I'll be there in a few minutes. See you then."

Joni's house was located in a lower middle-class neighborhood. There was an old camper in the driveway of the house and a boat in the side yard that was visible from the street. Liz parked in front of the house, which was kept up far better than the homes on either side. She and Winston got out of her van.

Interesting woman, Liz thought. *According to her brother she's willing to do what's necessary to cause a woman to miscarry, and yet she's obviously made an attempt to be a good housekeeper. Somehow, I don't think all of that fits. It will be interesting to see what I can learn about her.*

She rang the doorbell while Winston sat quietly at her side. A moment later she heard a voice ask, "Who is it?"

"It's Liz Lucas, Joni. I talked to you a few minutes ago about your granddaughter's birthday party."

The door was opened by a woman who appeared to be in her early fifties, approximately Liz's age, but the years had been a lot kinder to Liz. Joni had washed-out dishwater brown hair that was shot with grey, and had obviously not sought the help of a hair stylist or colorist.

She wore no makeup and was dressed in a cheap looking blouse which barely covered the bulging midriff she tried to hide by wearing dark colored polyester pants pulled up high above her waist.

Joni's face lit up when she saw Winston. "I didn't know you were bringing a dog. I love dogs, but Rocco, my husband, won't let me have one. Is it okay if I pet him?"

"Absolutely. His name is Winston, and I had to take him to the vet. That's why he's with me. If you don't want me to bring him into your house, I can leave him in my van."

"No. I'd love to have him come in. Rocco isn't allergic to dogs. He just doesn't like them. Guess one tried to bite him when he was a kid, and he's never gotten over it. Liz, Winston, please come in. Welcome to my home."

They followed Joni into one of the most comfortable homes Liz had ever been in. Joni clearly had a knack for making things, from the freshly baked apple bread Liz saw cooling on a rack in the kitchen to the needlepoint pillows that were scattered on chairs and sofas. The house was spotless. Obviously, Joni's home was a source of pride to her.

"Your home is lovely. You clearly have a knack for homemaking. I wish I had your talent."

"Thank you. We don't have a lot of money, so I've learned to make do with what I have, and I love to make things. I'm glad you like it. Please, have a seat and help yourself to some apple bread. I baked two loaves just a little while ago. Winston, come here and let me pet you." She gently stroked Winston and said, "I took a lot of pictures of my granddaughter's party, and I put them in an album. Would you like to see it?"

"I'd love to. This is going to save me so much time. Thank you." For the next twenty minutes Kelly enjoyed the apple bread and looked at the pictures while Joni pretty much planned Liz's make-believe child's birthday party.

Joni closed the last page of the album and turned to Liz. "Any questions?"

"Well, I do have one. That has to have been the best birthday party any little girl ever had. I'm totally intimidated, and based on what your brother told me, I'm amazed you were able to be so helpful to me."

"I'm sorry, but I don't know what you mean," Joni said in a perplexed voice.

"Your brother mentioned to me that your father had recently died, and that today it was determined that he'd been murdered. I'm so sorry. This must be hard for you."

A dark look flitted across Joni's face and then she said, "My father and I were estranged for many years. I was sorry when he died, but I was far sorrier that we never reconciled. As far as murder goes, yes, Larry called me and told me about the results of the autopsy. I guess my father's case has been reopened, and now the police are looking for the murderer."

"Your brother seems to think that the woman your father had been seeing had a motive for murdering him. He said she thought she could get her hands on the money her children would be entitled to under the law that was recently passed regarding children conceived after the father is deceased."

Joni turned away from Liz. When she did, the neckline on her blouse was pulled away from her neck, and Liz saw a dark red bruise. Liz knew enough from the cases that Roger had handled and the conversations they'd had regarding domestic abuse, that there was a good chance Joni was a victim. Her next words convinced Liz.

"Actually, I don't think Michelle did it. I honestly think she loved my father, and after the difficult marriage he and my mother had, I was happy for him, even if we were estranged. I know my brother hopes enough pressure will be put on her so she'll miscarry, and then we'll each get half of my father's estate. My husband feels the same way."

"Have you talked to the police and told them that?"

Joni became quite agitated and said, "No, I can't. I have my reasons."

Liz put her hand on Joni's arm and said, "Does the bruise on your neck have something to do with your decision?"

"What bruise?" Joni asked, unconsciously moving her hand up to cover her neck.

"The one on your neck," Liz said. "I know a little about domestic abuse, and I know this is none of my business, but if you feel you're in danger, I know someone who has the resources to help you."

"No, you're imagining things. There's been no domestic abuse. Anyway, Rocco didn't mean to do it," she said as she immediately covered her mouth, realizing what she had just said. "Really, Rocco's a wonderful husband. He grew up in a family where yelling and screaming was normal. He doesn't mean anything by it. No, we're just fine. You can ask Larry. They're really close."

"I'll respect your wishes, Joni, but I want to give you my cell phone number. If you ever want to call me, for any reason, please don't hesitate to do so." She knew there was nothing more she could do for Joni. She was just one of the legions of women who were so afraid of their husbands they would do anything to avoid suffering any more emotional or physical abuse.

Liz stood up and she and Winston walked over to the door. "Joni, thank you, and I wish you well. Remember, if you ever need a friend, I'm here." She opened the door and as she closed it, she could hear Joni softly crying.

CHAPTER TWENTY-FOUR

Promptly at 5:00 that afternoon, Liz walked into Walter Highsmith's office, accompanied by Winston. From the looks of the man standing outside the office door, she was certain that Roger had procured the services of bodyguards for Michelle. Liz was the last one there and was surprised when she saw Sean. He normally never attended meetings like this.

"I know I'm not late, so I'm going to assume that all of you are early," she said as she sat down next to Roger. Winston put his head on Roger's knee, indicating he could use a little petting, which Roger was happy to provide.

"Liz, we haven't even started. Roger told us that he'd told you about the results of the autopsy which indicated Bernie Spitzer didn't die from natural causes, but was in fact murdered. I asked Sean to sit in on this meeting, because there's a good chance Roger and I are going to need him to do some more research on the list of possible suspects. Of course, our main purpose here is to keep Michelle from being charged with murder. Who actually killed Bernie isn't really a priority of ours. Roger said you'd found out some information, and we'd all like to hear what you've discovered," Walter said.

Liz looked at the people who were seated in Walter's spacious office overlooking San Francisco, a view not that different from Roger's, which made perfect sense since they were both partners in the law firm, although they had different specialties. She noticed how pale looking Michelle was, and could only imagine the strain she was under.

"Walter, while you and Roger were dealing with the legal aspects concerning the findings of the autopsy, I was able to talk with three of the possible suspects." She looked over at Sean and said, "Once again, Sean, the information you gave me this morning was excellent. I was able to find all of them rather easily. It's always good to see you, but I thought your soccer team had practice tonight for the big game tomorrow."

"When Roger called with the autopsy information, I called my assistant coach, and he's taking the practice tonight. The boys will probably be happy I'm not there, because I'm a pretty ruthless when we're this close to a championship," he said laughing.

Liz turned back to the rest of them and said, "Let me start with Jim Brown. He wasn't in his apartment, but I happened to run into his next-door neighbor. Actually, Michelle, he's Joe, the doorman at your condominium building. I recognized him from when we were there last night."

"He's very nice," Michelle said. "I like him a lot. He's always doing special things for me, like bringing up a package that's been delivered to me rather than me having to go down and get it. I think he was working there when Bernie bought the condo for me several years ago."

"Probably. When I found out where he worked and that he was Jim Brown's neighbor, I became very suspicious. I thought it would be pretty easy for Jim to gain access to Bernie's condo through him."

"Liz, from the tone of your voice, I'm gathering you changed your mind about that," Roger said.

"Yes, I did. Here's what he told me." She recounted her conversation with Jim Brown and ended by saying, "After spending time with him, I'm absolutely convinced he didn't have anything to do with Bernie's death. He's in the advanced stage of pancreatic cancer, and from our conversation, I gathered that he'd decided to accept the part he played in his life's downward spiral. He even mentioned in the past he'd had thoughts of seeking revenge against Bernie Spitzer, but instead all his energy for the past few months had been focused on trying to stay alive. Poor man."

Roger had been taking notes the whole time Liz had been talking. He looked up and said, "I agree. I don't think he's worth spending time on. You said you'd met with three of the possible suspects. Who were the other two?"

"I was able to talk to, in person, both of Bernie's children, Larry and Joni."

"And?" Walter asked.

"I don't think his daughter had anything to do with it, and here's why." She told them about Joni's relationship with her father and how sad she was that she and Bernie had never reconciled prior to his death.

"Liz, I agree with your thoughts based on what you just told us, so that leaves her brother, Larry," Roger said.

"Yes, and there's one other person I think needs to be looked into and that's Joni's husband, Rocco Toscano. Sean, would you please tell the group what you told me about him?"

Sean relayed the information that Rocco was a go-to person for the Luchese crime family. He told them how Rocco had been charged with different crimes a number of times, but a good Mafia lawyer had always been able to get him off, and for that reason, he'd never been convicted of a crime.

"Sean concluded his presentation by saying, "hate to use this trite expression since the guy's never done time, but if it walks like a duck and it talks like a duck, it probably is a duck. At least that's my thinking. In other words, I'd be willing to bet everything I have that the guy's dirty."

"Tomorrow you might want to do a little more research," Liz said. "I know there were a couple of domestic abuse issues, but Joni refused to press charges. I think those are probably valid as well, because she had a nasty bruise on her neck. I talked to her about domestic abuse and how we could help her, but she wasn't having any of it. Like so many women, the known is a little easier to accept than the scary unknown. I think Rocco needs to be looked at very closely. I don't need to remind you that the people he works for have the means to commit murder. Maybe Rocco got one of them to kill Bernie."

Roger turned to Sean and said, "Make that a priority tomorrow morning. That's an angle I haven't really considered."

Michelle reached for her purse and took out her ringing cell phone. "Excuse me, this is Dr. Throckmorton. I called him earlier and asked for a prescription. I'll be back in a minute." She walked towards the door and as she entered the hallway they heard her say, "This is Michelle D'Amato, Doctor."

CHAPTER TWENTY-FIVE

Almost as soon as Michelle left the room, the phone on Walter's large teak desk rang. Since he'd told his secretary to leave when all of the people for the meeting had arrived, she wasn't around to take his calls.

"Excuse me," he said. "Cheryl's gone for the evening, so I better take this call." A moment later they heard him say, "This is Walter Highsmith."

He was quiet as he listened to the voice on the other end of the phone and then he said, "Thank you, Detective. I'm in a meeting right now with her attorney, and I'll pass this information on to him."

He hung up the phone and turned to Roger. "That was Detective Latham. Unfortunately, he called to tell me that he's planning on interviewing Michelle tomorrow. The coroner has determined that uncommonly large amounts of the poison known as propofol, were found in Bernie's body. Are you familiar with the drug? I'm not."

"Nor am I. Sean, there's some more research. Find out who has access to it, what it's used for, and how it's administered. That's a priority right up there with Rocco.'

"Got it, Boss."

Just then the door opened and a very shaken Michelle walked into the room, her eyes brimming with tears. Walter hurried over to her and led her to the couch. "Michelle, what is it? Are you all right?" he asked.

She was quiet for several moments, tears coursing down her cheeks. Even in her obvious pain, she was still beautiful. Liz thought she had to be the only woman she'd ever known who could cry and still look like she was ready for a photo shoot.

Finally, she began to speak, "I don't know what's happening. That was Dr. Throckmorton on the phone. He wanted to tell me he'd called in a prescription to my pharmacy for me." She paused and took a tissue from her purse.

"I'm sorry, Michelle, but somehow I'm missing the connection between you crying and the doctor saying he'd called in a prescription for you," Roger said.

"That's not why I'm crying. It was what he said after that," she said as she wiped the tears from her eyes. "He said I hadn't mentioned anything about the $500,000 I owed him. I told him I didn't know what he was talking about."

"He said you owed him $500,000?" Roger asked incredulously.

"Yes. Then he told me it was very clear in the papers I'd signed right before I'd undergone the artificial insemination process." She started to cry again.

"Michelle, did you sign papers before you underwent the procedure?" Walter asked.

"I don't think I did, but I don't remember much about that day. Quite frankly, I was so excited and intent on the procedure, I didn't pay much attention to anything else."

"Well, it's things like that that keep a lot of us lawyers in business," Walter said drily. "When you indicated you didn't know what he was talking about, what did he say?"

"He said he needed to see me so we could talk about it. I have an appointment to see him tomorrow at 5:00 in the evening. He said the only reason I was pregnant was because he was able to convince Bernie to donate his sperm, and once the babies were born, according to the document I'd signed, I owed him big time, to the tune of $500,000. He said my babies were going to be very wealthy, because according to a recent law that had been passed, they were entitled to their share of Bernie's estate. He said I could easily afford to pay him the money I'd agreed to when I signed the papers in his office."

The men exchanged looks, and it was Sean who spoke up first. "Michelle, what did you say your doctor's name was? I'd like to do a quick search and see what I can find out about him before we finish up this meeting. Roger, if I'm not back when you're ready to wind things up, give me a call. I should be able to find something out," Sean said, as he hurried out the door.

"All right, Michelle, let's put that on the back burner until Sean returns. Liz, you still have one more person you met with. I believe that's Larry Spitzer. What did you find out about him?" Roger asked.

"He was just leaving his apartment when I got there, and I followed him. He went into a local neighborhood bar, and when I saw that there was a patio area, I took Winston in with me, hoping they'd allow dogs on the patio." She smiled at Roger and said, "See, I told you I was being safe."

She continued. "In my opinion, I think Larry should still be considered a suspect. He told me he was going to be coming into a lot of money pretty soon." She stopped talking and turned to Walter.

"Walter, I really would prefer it if Michelle didn't hear what he had to say. I don't think she needs this right now." She faced Michelle and said, "You're not in any danger, but I'm a big believer in limiting the negative things a mother-to-be hears when she's pregnant. Why don't you step outside for a minute? I know words are just that, nothing but words, but no use hearing words that might not be pleasant. Will you do me a favor and humor me?"

Michelle looked at Walter who nodded in agreement, and then stepped into the hallway, closing the door behind her.

Liz resumed speaking. "Larry said he was sure Michelle was the murderer, and that the pressure of her being under investigation and probably found guilty of murder would be enough to cause her to lose the babies. He also said when he gets his inheritance he plans on buying the most expensive breed of dog on the market, an Argentine Mastiff, and living in a penthouse. I have no idea if he's the murderer, but I wonder if he and Joni's husband, Rocco, could have planned it, because Larry and Joni were the heirs. Little did they know there would soon be two additional heirs."

Everyone sat quietly for a moment then Roger said, "Liz, did you get a sense of Larry's mental or emotional condition? When Sean sent me the information he'd found on everyone, there was quite a bit about Larry's drug and alcohol problems, and as I recall, he'd even been arrested. Did you see any evidence of that?"

"Not anything to do with drugs, but yes, alcohol, that very well could be. When I got to the patio area of the bar, the barmaid had already brought him a beer. She obviously knew what kind he drank. He bought the beer I ordered and told the barmaid to put it on his tab. Both of those things tell me he frequents the bar. He also said he had an ironclad alibi for the night Bernie was murdered. He said he was with a bunch of men at a meeting. When he left he said he had to meet his sponsor, then he put a handful of breath mints in his mouth. I don't know if he was going to AA meetings or what, but it sure sounded like it to me."

"I'll have Sean see if he's under a court mandate to attend meetings. I know from Sean's information that he's been arrested several times for being intoxicated in public, so it might have something to do with that. As far as his and Rocco's relationship, that's something else I'll ask Sean to check on in the morning."

"Is there anything else you found relevant about Larry?" Walter asked.

"No. That's about it. Even if he didn't do it, I wonder if he and Rocco were somehow in it together."

"Can I tell Michelle she can come back in now?" Walter asked. "I hate for her to be out there wondering what's being said about her."

"Yes, you're absolutely right, Walter. The last thing she needs right now is anything else to worry about," Roger said

He opened the door and told Michelle to come back in, and at the same time saw Sean hurrying down the hall towards Walter's office with a grim look on his face.

CHAPTER TWENTY-SIX

Michelle walked into the room, followed by Sean, and they both sat down. Sean had several sheets of paper in his hand.

"Michelle we're finished with the conversations Liz had with three of the suspects, and now I'd like to see if Sean was able to find out anything about Dr. Throckmorton," Walter said. They all turned and looked at Sean.

"I found out quite a bit, and Michelle, if I were your attorney, and I'm not, I'd advise you to get a new doctor right away. This one has a lot of baggage, and he looks really dirty to me."

"Sean, I'm not sure I've ever heard you refer to anyone in such strong words or with that tone of voice. What have you found out?" Roger asked, looking over at Michelle, who had an ashen look on her face.

Walter had been watching her as well. He poured a glass of water from the carafe on the table in front of them and handed it to her. "I don't know much about pregnancy, but it might be a good idea if you took a deep breath and drank this. Based on the way Sean looks right now, you might need it."

"First of all, Dr. Throckmorton is deeply in debt. I mean really deeply in debt, to the tune of almost losing his multi-million-dollar house in Richmond. The bank has come very close to foreclosing on it several times. He's been married numerous times and his present wife was a wannabe starlet in Mexico. He met her on the beach and brought her to the United States as his wife ten days later. I found a photo of her, and she's a knockout, but according to the records I saw, she could singlehandedly win the grand prize for being the queen of charge cards."

"Sean, I think I remember seeing a picture of her on the doctor's desk, and I have to agree with you," Michelle said. "She really is a beauty."

"Not only a beauty, a much younger beauty with very expensive tastes. Word has it that the doctor is concerned she'll find someone younger and leave him. Dr. Throckmorton is about twenty-five years older than she is."

"What about the fertility clinic he runs? I agree that having big debts could lead him to develop a scheme to have unsuspecting patients sign papers essentially giving him $500,000 for babies to be successfully conceived and born, but that means to me that the fertility clinic is at the crux of this," Roger said.

"You're right, and that's where he's dirty, or at least allegedly dirty. He runs a fertility clinic, as we know, and in addition, a sperm bank which freezes the sperm of men who wish for a woman to bear their child at a later date. It's become a pretty 'big' thing in the last few years, because many of the military servicemen who go to war are afraid they will suffer injuries that will leave them unable to have children. Using a sperm bank allows them to have children if they suffer such injuries or are even killed in action. Naturally, Dr. Throckmorton charges a hefty price for this service."

"I believe it became popular after a recent law in California was passed that provides when a child is conceived using the sperm of a man that is already deceased, then that child is entitled to receive an inheritance from the deceased father's estate. The intent of the law was to help the widows of servicemen who died serving their country, but like to many laws, it has had some unintended consequences which have led to abuses by individuals such as Dr. Throckmorton."

"Wait a minute, Sean. That law is the reason Bernie's soon to be born children will be able to inherit part of his estate," Michelle said.

"I realize that, Michelle, and I'm not downplaying how important it can be to someone like you who wanted to have a man's child or children for the right reasons. What I'm saying is that when a law such as this one exists, the darker side of human nature comes out, and it can be abused. I believe that's what's happened here."

"Sean, please continue," Roger said. "I haven't heard anything yet that leads me to believe Dr. Throckmorton could have something to do with Bernie's death other than the fact that he was the intermediary for Michelle becoming pregnant."

"Just listen to me, Roger. Although he's called 'Dr. T' by his adoring patients, and there are many of them, the California Department of Health Care Services has a different view of him. They've investigated him several times for improper practices and fraud. Several women have filed complaints with the Department, alleging that Dr. Throckmorton made them sign papers indicating they were to pay him large sums of money upon the successful birth of a child. Although they filed complaints, in every instance they withdrew their complaints after they gave birth. I couldn't find out whether they were paid off or just so happy they had a child that they decided to let it go."

Roger's face was stony. "Sean, were you able to find out how much money the doctor requested they pay him?"

"I was in a hurry, so I only examined a couple of complaints filed with the Department. They were five figure sums. Not huge, but substantial enough that someone would have to be a person of means to pay him."

"Sean, do you know if his practice caters to wealthy women?" Walter asked.

"I tried to follow up on that angle, Walter, but none of my information gave me demographics regarding the income levels of his patients. I'll see what I can find out tomorrow regarding the answer to that question."

Michelle spoke up. "I might be able to help. Obviously, I've been in his office a number of times, and each time the waiting room has been filled with women and occasionally their husbands or a man was with them. Almost all of them were expensively dressed and wearing what I considered to be high priced jewelry. From what I observed, I would have to say his practice is definitely made up of wealthy women who could well afford to pay what he asked."

The five of them were quiet for several minutes, trying to determine if there was a nexus between Dr. Throckmorton and Bernie Spitzer's murder. Walter was the first to speak.

"Roger, I know that criminal defense is your area, not mine. I do family law and estate issues, but I'm having some real problems with this. I'm spinning out a fantasy in my mind that this doctor got Michelle to sign some papers, or possibly even forged her signature, and now expects her to pay him $500,000 when the twins are born. I am really, really uncomfortable about her going to his office alone tomorrow. I know this is a huge stretch, but what if he's the murderer? What if he murdered Bernie so he could get his hands on $500,000?" Walter asked.

Again, the room was very quiet as each one of them thought about the implications of Walter's statements.

"I hate to be an alarmist, but I found out a few other things that are causing me some concern, and I'm sure all of you will feel the same way when you hear it," Sean said.

"Sean, for Pete's sake, don't leave us hanging. Out with it." Walter said.

"Okay, here goes. You know it was determined that Bernie's death was caused by the drug Propofol. Well, he was in pretty good company, because it's also the same drug that caused Michael Jackson's death. Although Jackson's death was accidental, the doctor who administered a deadly overdose of Propofol to him was subsequently convicted of murder, in the form of involuntary manslaughter. So, this drug is not only dangerous, but obviously, it can kill."

"That's where I've heard the name. I've been racking my brain ever since I got the call from Detective Latham. I was going to do some research on it later," Walter said.

"I'll save you the time," Sean said. "This is a drug that's used primarily by anesthesiologists as a sedative, but obviously in large quantities it can cause death, just as it did to Michael Jackson. It's also used for migraines and in many surgical procedures requiring some minor sedation. I would bet my next pay check that Dr. Throckmorton has a supply of it in his office."

"Sean, in a roundabout way, are you implying that Dr. Throckmorton murdered Bernie?" Michelle asked incredulously.

"I'm not a lawyer or a judge, Michelle. I simply do the research and let other people make determinations." He looked first at Walter and then at Roger, then he spoke directly to Michelle, "Although I'm not an attorney, if I were, I'd make sure you had someone with you when you meet with Dr. Throckmorton tomorrow evening."

CHAPTER TWENTY-SEVEN

"All right, I've heard enough," Walter said. "I'm calling Detective Latham and telling him what we've found out. This is his case and like Sean said, if Michelle is going to go to that meeting tomorrow evening, I want to make darn sure she's protected. Roger, I know she's your client in this aspect of the case, so I better ask your permission to call him. And quite frankly, asking you is just a courtesy on my part." He turned towards Michelle. "Michelle, I promise you that if you keep that meeting tomorrow evening, you will be protected one way or another at all times. Nothing is going to happen to you or your babies."

Walter walked over to his desk and picked up the phone. A few minutes later, they heard him say, "Detective Latham, this is Walter Highsmith, regarding the Bernie Spitzer case. I have some information that is extremely relevant to the case. In fact, I might be able to give you the name of the murderer. I know it's late, but could you come to my office right now? I'm in a meeting with some people who have shared some important information about the case with me."

He was quiet as he listened to the detective. "Yes, I understand. We'll be here. Do you need the address of my law office?" He listened again and said, "Fine. We'll be waiting for you. Thank you." He turned and said, "Let's take a break. He's on his way, but he said with rush hour traffic, it might take a little while for him to get here.

The police department isn't that far away, so I think he'll be here in about thirty minutes or so. I have some soft drinks and fruit in the refrigerator in the back room. Help yourself."

Walter's estimate had been absolutely right. Thirty minutes later the detective knocked on the door and then opened it. Walter knew Detective Latham, and he introduced him to the others, although he had met Michelle briefly the night Bernie died. He pulled a chair over for the detective.

"Mitch, this might take a little while. First of all, I'd like Liz to give you a recap of her conversations with Bernie's two adult children as well as Jim Brown, the man who founded Spitzer Electronics with Bernie many years ago. I know all of these people are on your list of suspects, as well as Michelle here. Based on what you're about hear this evening, I think you'll agree that she should no longer be considered a suspect."

"You've certainly whetted my curiosity, Walter. Mrs. Langley, I'd very much like to hear what you've found out."

Liz spent the next twenty minutes giving an abbreviated version of her conversations with Larry, Joni, and Jim Brown to Detective Latham. When she was finished, Walter said, "Mitch, there's more. Sean is a private investigator who has worked for our firm for many years. He's done some research, actually it's pretty quick research, since we didn't give him much time, on a Dr. Jerome Throckmorton. I don't know if you've run across his name."

"No. That's a completely new name to me. Are you telling me that he should be considered as a suspect in the Spitzer murder?"

"I'll let you decide. First I'd like Michelle to tell you about a telephone conversation she had with the doctor earlier this evening." He nodded towards Michelle. "Michelle, please tell the doctor what you told us about the prescription, the $500,000 the doctor said you will owe him when the twins are born, and the meeting he's requesting for tomorrow evening."

"The doctor said you'd owe him $500,000 when the twins are born? That's a lot of money," the detective said. "Whatever for?"

Michelle related the conversation she'd had with Dr. Throckmorton earlier that evening in detail. When she was finished, he was quiet and then he said, "We have a detective on the force who deals exclusively with fraud in the medical community. I have to say I don't know that much about it. I'll give him a call and see what I can find out. Is there more?"

"Actually, quite a bit, Mitch. I'll let Sean tell you what he found out about the doctor and when you speak to your contact, see what he thinks about it. Sean, please tell the detective what you were able to find out."

Sean began to speak and even though the others in the room had heard it before, they were just as rapt hearing it for the second time as they had been the first time. He concluded by saying, "Detective, I'd really like to know what your expert has to say about what I've just told you. If he'd like to know where I found the information, if it's something I can share with him, I'd be happy to."

Detective Latham sat for a long time, deep in thought, and then he said, "Mr. Langley, Walter, I understand that both of you represent Mrs. D'Amato, although for different things, is that correct?"

"Yes," Walter answered. "I'm representing her regarding her petitioning the court for a family allowance during her pregnancy, and when her twins are born, I will be representing the twins to claim their share of Bernie Spitzer's estate. Roger is representing her as far as any legal defense that may be required in connection with the murder of Bernie Spitzer."

"So, it's fair for me to say both of you would more or less be representing her when she has her meeting with Dr. Throckmorton tomorrow evening. Would that be correct?"

Michelle spoke up. "Detective, I'm not going to attend the

meeting. I can't be alone with that man knowing what I now know. What if he decides to do something to me? It's after hours, and no one will be in his office."

"I'm well aware of that Ms. D'Amato. Believe me, I'll make sure that nothing happens to you, however I think it's critical for you to attend that meeting for a number of reasons. He just went to the top of my list of suspects, but let me remind you of something. Dr. Throckmorton needs you to be healthy so you can deliver the twins, and he can get the $500,000 he's demanding from you. I will give you my word that absolutely nothing is going to happen to you. I intend to have several of my men nearby, and I will be there as well. Believe me, you'll be as safe as you've ever been. I need to figure out exactly how I want to do this, not only for your safety, but so we can have a record of everything that takes place during that meeting."

"How do you intend to do that?" Michelle asked, doubt written all over her face.

"I don't know yet. I'll definitely want you to wear a recording device, but I need to figure out what would be the best one for you. Am I correct that this is not a medical examination, but simply a meeting in his office?"

"Yes, there's no reason for an exam. He examined me right after the results of the ultrasound showed that I was pregnant with twins and said everything was fine."

"In that case, we could conceal a recording device in your clothing or mount it in your jewelry. I'd like to meet with all of you tomorrow afternoon and work out the details. I also want my friend to look over what Sean has and see what else he can find, if anything. It's getting late, and mothers-to-be need their beauty sleep, or so my wife told me when she was pregnant. Does anyone have any questions?" he asked as he looked around the room at each of them.

"I do. I know this probably sounds silly, but I'm scared to be alone with him, and I don't think he'll let anyone else be in the room with me if we're going to talk about me paying him $500,000,"

Michelle said.

"I understand your concern, but let me reiterate that I'm sure the doctor wouldn't do anything to hurt you or your babies," the detective said. "It's in his best interests to make sure nothing happens to you."

"That's easy for you to say. You won't be the one in the room alone with someone who may be a murderer." Michelle folded her arms, and she looked at Walter for support.

There was silence in the room as they all recognized the truth of her words. Liz broke the silence by saying, "Detective Latham. I may have a solution to the problem."

"If you do, I think we'd all like to hear it," he said.

"I won't go into the details, but I've been involved in the investigation of several murder cases. I have no formal training, it just seemed I happened to be there when murders were involved. Before Roger and I were married, a murder occurred at the spa I own, The Red Cedar Lodge and Spa. Roger became concerned for my safety since he was working in San Francisco, and I was in Red Cedar. He bought Winston for me," Liz said as she nodded towards Winston, who was lying on the floor next to Roger. When he heard his name, Winston stood up and put his head on Liz's lap.

"That's a beautiful dog, Mrs. Langley, but I fail to see what this has to do with Michelle," Detective Latham said.

"I'm getting there. Roger bought him from a trainer who specializes in guard dogs. His name is Ed James. You may have heard of him."

The detective interrupted her, "Of course, I know him. The department buys all of their dogs from him. He's the best in the business." He turned to Roger and said, "That must have set you back a bit. His dogs don't come cheap."

"It was the best investment I ever made," Roger said. "Winston has been responsible for saving Liz's life several times, and you can't put a price on that."

"I'm getting the sense that your solution to Michelle being by herself in the doctor's office has something to do with Winston. Would that be correct?"

"That it would. As you know, all of the James dogs are trained both in verbal commands and touch commands. I was thinking that Michelle could take Winston home with her tonight. If I say it's all right, Winston will go with her. That way they could establish a bond. Michelle could tell the doctor that she's been seeing a psychiatrist, and the psychiatrist recommended that Michelle get a comfort dog. Winston will be the comfort dog, and I imagine the doctor will allow him to accompany Michelle into his office."

"All right. So far, I'm liking the plan. Then what?"

"I'll spend some time with Michelle tomorrow showing her different touch commands for Winston. If she feels threatened in any way, Winston will instantly react to her command, and I assume that you and your men will be close enough by that you could be in the doctor's office in a matter of minutes, if not seconds." She turned to Michelle and said, "Would that make you feel safer?"

"Yes. When I was at your spa several months ago, I'd often go up to the lodge just to see Winston. You may remember as soon as I entered the room this evening, he walked over to me. I'd love to have him spend the night with me. Thank you. I think that solves my problem."

"Detective, how does that sound to you?" Michelle asked.

"I think it will work. Let me figure out a few more details. I'd like to meet here at 3:00 tomorrow afternoon. That will give me time to go over whatever else I've found out and prepare you for the meeting with the doctor."

He looked around the room and they all nodded, then Walter spoke. "Mitch, however you decide to play this, I want to be involved. I recognize the doctor probably wouldn't allow me to go into the room with Michelle, but I want to be with your men."

"So do I," Roger said, "and I think one of the bodyguards I hired for her should be there as well."

"I'll accompany Michelle to his office and stay out in the reception area. I want to be a part of this, too," Liz said.

Detective Latham looked over at Sean and said, "Looks like it's beginning to get a little crowded. I suppose you want to be in on this as well?"

"Nope, I coach my nephew's soccer team, and we have a huge game tomorrow night. If we win it, we'll be league champions. You'd probably be investigating another murder if I asked my assistant to take that game," Sean said laughing. "However, I'll be here at three tomorrow, and I plan on doing some more research as well."

"All right now that it's decided, do you think Winston would let me take him for a walk when I take Michelle home?" Walter asked. "After the day she's had, I think she needs to rest."

"Yes, let me give him a couple of commands." She petted Winston and said, "Winston, guard Michelle. Guard Michelle," and at the same time pointed with her hand towards Michelle. The big boxer immediately stood up and walked over to Michelle, sitting next to her. Liz turned to Walter. "Walter, walk over to Winston and hold out your hand. Let him sniff it. When he licks it, reach down and pet him."

Walter went over to Winston, and a moment later Liz said, "Winston, guard Walter, guard Walter. That should take care of it for tonight. If you have any questions, give me a call. Michelle, I have one favor to ask of you. Do not let Winston sleep with you. He sleeps outside our bedroom, and he can do the same with you."

"Uh-huh, sure Liz," Michelle said, and Liz knew with certainty where Winston would be spending the night.

Oh well, Michelle has enough on her mind and since Winston is now a comfort dog, if it comforts her, what's one night sleeping on a nice soft bed with Michelle?

CHAPTER TWENTY-EIGHT

Roger pulled onto the freeway and said, "Liz, it's going to feel strange not to have Winston with us, but I think you did the right thing."

"It was the only thing I could think to do. On one hand, Dr. Throckmorton, whether he's the murderer or not, needs Michelle to be healthy so she can deliver those twins, but on the other hand, being alone with a possible murderer is not something I would recommend."

"Given the murders you've been involved in, and how many times you've been alone with murderers, I think you're more than well-qualified to speak on the subject, although it's one I wish you weren't so knowledgeable about," Roger said with a touch of irony.

"If it's any consolation to you, I feel the same way. The doctor is certainly not going to want any witnesses about Michelle paying him $500,000 when her twins are born, particularly if the person with her looks like a lawyer or someone involved in law enforcement."

Roger took his eyes off the road for a moment and said, "Liz, do you think I look like a lawyer?"

"Absolutely. I could pick you out of a lineup. Quite frankly, the vest you usually wear when you're seeing clients kind of gives you away, not to mention a few other things."

"Like what?"

"You know how you just know a guy's a cop because he has a mustache. Well, lawyers just look a certain way, too."

"Liz, I'm really surprised to hear you say that. I've heard you mention on a number of occasions that you're totally against profiling, and if that isn't profiling, I don't know what is."

"I disagree. If every time you've met someone who belongs to a certain group of people and they share one thing, when you see a person who has that particular thing, of course you're going to think they're part of that group."

Roger frowned. "Actually, I don't think we're getting anywhere with this conversation. Let's get back to Michelle and Bernie's death. What's your take on everything we heard tonight? You always have interesting insights, at least other than profiling insights, so I would like to know what you think."

Liz was quiet for several moments and then said, "I think the doctor certainly has a motive, what with being in debt, and trying to please his beautiful wife. His means of income will be placed in jeopardy if he's ever found guilty of committing blackmail in his infertility practice. Of course, that's not even addressing what would happen to his income if he goes to prison. If you combine those issues, it leaves me one central thought, he's desperate, and yes, he should be considered dangerous."

"For the sake of argument," Roger said, "let's say the doctor is found guilty of murdering Bernie Spitzer. Here's the interesting part. If, in fact, Michelle did sign a valid contract agreeing to give him $500,000 upon the healthy delivery of her babies, even if he's in prison, contractually he could still legally receive the money. In the eyes of the law, a contract is a contract, and the courts will enforce it."

Liz gasped. "Seriously, Roger? That doesn't sound right. And another thing you just said would cause anyone to know you're a lawyer."

"What's that?"

"When you said 'for the sake of argument.' Lawyers always want to have the last word in an argument."

"I'm not even going to address that. Let's get back to the contract Michelle might have signed. It may not sound right, but that's the law. We have to impress upon Detective Latham and everyone else how critical it is for Michelle to get a copy of that contract. First of all, I'd like to see if one even exists. Secondly, if she did sign it, was it under duress, although since she doesn't even remember signing it, that probably isn't going to work. Thirdly, if her signature is on it, is it really her signature?"

"What do you mean? Do you think the doctor might have forged her signature?" Liz asked.

"That's a possibility, but there's another one that sounds less risky. I've never heard of a doctor operating on someone or even doing a minor in-office procedure without the patient signing a consent form. I think a doctor's malpractice insurance carrier would have an apoplectic fit if such a form wasn't signed. Maybe Michelle signed a consent form just before the procedure, and afterwards he attached the signed consent form with her signature on it to the contract. It's been my experience that people almost never read a consent form in that type of situation."

"Well if that's the case, how would you ever prove what she signed really wasn't what she thought it was?"

"That's why Walter made the comment, that's what keeps lawyers in business. It's also why I always tell my clients to read every word before they sign anything. Ah, home sweet home," he said as he turned up the lane leading to the Red Cedar Lodge and Spa. "It's really late, and I had a sandwich from Walter's refrigerator, but I'm in the mood for something tasty. Got any ideas?"

"With a little luck, there will be a couple of extra pieces of the black and white cheesecake Gina was going to make for dinner tonight. Keep your fingers crossed that the guests didn't have seconds." Roger parked his car, and they both climbed out.

"I'd hope not," Roger grumbled. "I'd think if you wanted to go to a spa you'd a least try to eat healthily, and two pieces of cheesecake doesn't sound real healthy to me."

"Agreed."

They walked into the great room of the lodge, and Liz headed towards the kitchen to check the refrigerator and see if there was any cheesecake left. A moment later she called out to Roger who was looking at his email. "You must be living right. There are two pieces of cheesecake with our names on them. I'll plate them and put them on the counter."

As Roger finished the last of the cheesecake, he let out a long sigh.

"What was that for?" Liz asked.

"I'm just feeling sad that there isn't another piece. Since I'm not a guest at the spa I could have justified two pieces."

"It's probably better for your lawyer look that there isn't," she grinned as she reached over and patted his stomach which constantly threatened to expand because of her cooking.

"Okay, I get the hint. Let's get back to Michelle's case. I think you should accompany her. Even though she'll have Winston with her, she's still going to be nervous. You'll need to keep her as calm as possible."

Liz pushed the crumbs around on her plate. "I'm planning on it. I'll call her in the morning to see how she's doing, but I thought I'd go to her condo about 1:00 tomorrow afternoon. That will give me plenty of time to show her the commands for Winston, although I hope she doesn't have to use them. And I really hate to miss another dinner here at the lodge. I'm worried Gina will quit because of the extra work I've put on her. At the least, I need to give her a bonus for doing all of this."

"I don't think she's going to quit. From what she's told me she loves working here. She even told me once her favorite times are when she gets to do everything by herself, because she feels like she's the owner of the spa and everybody always compliments her on the food she prepares."

"She said that to you?" Liz asked with an incredulous look on her face.

"Yes," Roger said, grinning. "We were talking a few weeks ago, so I don't think you have anything to worry about. Of course, I could start worrying that she won't ever make that cheesecake again, and that would probably cause me some sleepless nights."

"I think your beauty sleep is safe, since I promise I'll make it for you in the very near future."

"I'd prefer it if you gave me a specific date, so I'd have something to look forward to," Roger said with a plaintive look on his face.

"Tell you what. If it will cause you to sleep better, I'll make it as soon as this issue with Michelle is resolved. How does that sound?"

"Does that mean if it's over tomorrow night, you'll make it the next day?" he asked hopefully.

"Yep. A promise is a promise."

"Okay, now that we've solved that problem, we probably need to get some sleep. I have a feeling tomorrow is going to be a very interesting day," he said as he picked up their plates and carried them over to the sink.

"I just hope it's a good interesting and not bad interesting," Liz said, getting up from her seat and following him. "I really am concerned about how much stress Michelle can take without it having some effect on her and the babies." She rinsed the plates, put them in the dishwasher, and started it.

Fifteen minutes later when they were in bed and Liz was almost asleep, Roger said, "I'm having trouble getting to sleep. I'm used to knowing that Winston is right outside the door."

Liz put her head on his shoulder and said, "Pretend I'm Winston, and I got in bed with you. I have a feeling that's exactly what he's doing right now at Michelle's home."

CHAPTER TWENTY-NINE

Liz spent the next morning catching up on her email, meeting with Bertha, her manager, to see what had been happening with the spa during the last few days while she'd been gone, and writing instructions for Gina about the evening's dinner. She looked at the clock and knew that Gina was usually home at that time. She picked up her phone and called her.

Gina answered the phone in her usual cheery tone. Liz marveled that the young woman never seemed to have had a grumpy day in her life. "Hi Liz, how are you?"

"I'm fine, Gina, but I'm feeling really guilty about leaving you to do everything the last couple of days, and unfortunately, I'm going to have to go into the city again today, and I'll be there during dinner tonight. I'm so sorry, but something has come up."

"Liz, I understand, and knowing you, I rather imagine it has something to do with a murder. Actually, I enjoy preparing the dinners, and from what the guests have told me, I think it's gone well. As good as you are to me, I'm just happy to be able to help you."

"Thanks, I appreciate it. I think tonight will be the last time I have to ask you to fill in for me, at least for the near future. I've written out instructions and done some prep work, so you should be okay.

Unless something unforeseen happens, I'll see you tomorrow."

"Not to worry. Good luck with whatever it is you're doing," Gina said as she ended the call.

Liz punched in Michelle's telephone number on her cell phone, and it was answered almost immediately. "Liz, I can't tell you how much I love Winston. I hope you don't mind, but I did let him on my bed last night, and you know what? I slept like a baby. I wish I could keep him. He's wonderful. It's almost as if he knows what I'm thinking."

"Glad to hear that you like him, but I think I'd have a divorce to contend with if I gave him to you. Roger had a hard time getting to sleep last night without Winston. He's really become a part of our family. To change the subject, I was hoping we could meet at your condo at 1:00 this afternoon. I want to go over the touch commands for Winston with you, and then I can drive you to the meeting in Walter's office. After that I'll go to the doctor's office with you, and as we discussed last night, I'll wait in the doctor's reception area while you meet with him in his office. Would that be all right?"

"Yes, that's fine," Michelle said. "I was just getting ready to pan fry a steak I found in the freezer. We forgot about dog food, and I thought Winston might like that. I also have some hamburger I'm defrosting. Is that okay with you? I don't want him to starve."

Liz laughed. "You are really spoiling him. As a matter of fact, I did give Walter a couple of baggies of dog food, but I guess in the excitement of everything, they got overlooked. They're probably still in his office, and I'm sure Winston would prefer your treats over his daily dog food. I don't think you should be walking him. Is there someone there who can do it for you?"

"Yes, I told you I know the doorman, and he was more than happy to take Winston out early this morning when he got off work. My weekly cleaning lady came today, and she's taken him out as well. I'll have her do it one more time before you get here. Do you think that's enough?"

"More than enough. He'll be fine. How are you doing?"

"I'm okay. I'd probably be a blithering idiot if Winston wasn't here. Having something to do is keeping my mind off of the meeting. Quite frankly, I'm dreading it."

"I don't blame you, but remember, Winston will be with you at all times, and I have a feeling a lot of other people are going to be only seconds away. I've got a few more things to do before I leave. See you soon."

*****

Later that afternoon Liz walked into the lobby of Michelle's condominium building and immediately noticed the large bouquet of fresh flowers that was on the round table in the center of it. The other evening when she'd been at Michelle's she was so focused on Michelle and everything that was happening, she hadn't paid much attention to anything else. She decided then and there that a large vase of fresh flowers would be perfect on the table in the great room at her lodge. Zack, her gardener, made sure fresh flowers were always in the cottages, but she'd never thought to display a large bouquet in the lodge.

She took the elevator up to Michelle's floor, opened it, and was immediately greeted by a very happy Winston. He wagged his tail, sat down, and extended his paw, as Ed James, the dog trainer, had taught him to do when he first met people. Liz could only assume Michelle had told him she would be coming up on the elevator. She looked down the hall and saw Michelle standing in the doorway of her condo, grinning while a muscular young man, who she assumed was one of the bodyguards Roger had hired, stood next to it.

"Liz, are you sure I can't have that big guy?" Michelle asked while looking at her with a fake pout. "Since I'm going to come into some money while I'm receiving a family allowance from Bernie's estate, I'd pay you a ridiculous price for him."

"Fraid he's not for sale," Liz said as she and Winston walked through the doorway, "but you might consider getting a dog of your own. I'd be happy to give you the trainer's name. Roger spoke so highly of him and there's no doubt about it, Winston's the most highly trained dog I've ever seen. By the way, how did he like the steak and hamburger?"

"Considering he ate all of both of them, and then looked at me expectantly, I'd say he thoroughly enjoyed them, although I do have one little problem."

"What's that?" Liz said sitting down and scratching one of Winston's ears.

"My cleaning lady has fallen in love with him. She said she had a boxer when she was a little girl and always wanted another one, but her husband is allergic to dogs, so she can't have one."

"Doesn't sound like a problem to me."

"If your cleaning lady had spent the better part of the morning playing with a dog, brushing it, and not getting the things done I'm paying her to do, you might think it was a problem," Michelle said.

Liz laughed. "Well, I consider that a good problem. A bad problem would be if she hated dogs or she was the one who was allergic to dogs."

"I hadn't thought of that. I guess you're right. Okay, so now what?"

"I want to teach you two touch commands that Ed James showed me. The first one involves putting thumb pressure on Winston's right side, or his haunch. It's where his back leg and his rear meet. I'm going to point it out to you, but I'm not going to actually press there." She reached over and petted Winston and let her hand slide to that area. "Right in here is the trigger point. Don't ask me how, but the trainer said it must be done with the thumb. See?"

"Yes. That looks pretty easy. Why the thumb?"

"He told me that people always pet a dog with their hands, and no one would deliberately put a thumb there."

"That makes sense," Michelle said. "Now the question is, what does he do if someone puts their thumb in that region and presses?"

"It's a silent command for him to attack. By that, I mean a full-on attack, like taking a big bite out of the person who is the threat. Hopefully, the doctor won't do anything to earn that."

"No one hopes that more than I do." Michelle said as she nervously chewed on her lip. "What's the second command, and what's it for?"

"The second silent command is to press your knuckle under his chin, hard. If that's done to him, that's the command to take the person down. In other words, Winston won't bite him, but he'll pin him to the ground."

Michelle was quiet for several minutes and then she said, "How did he come up with those two touch commands?"

"I asked him the same question and was told that both of them can be done as if someone was simply petting Winston. The person who was to be the recipient of the command wouldn't be aware that I or someone else was doing anything other than simply petting him, which would seem very non-threatening."

"Wow." Her face lit up. "That's sheer genius. I guess it must have involved a lot of training to get Winston to learn that, but then again, as smart as he is, probably not."

"I don't know. Are you clear on these two commands? I can go over them again, if you'd like me to. I want you to feel safe."

"Thanks to you, Liz, I've never felt safer." Michelle looked at her, her eyes shining. "I'll have Winston sit next to me, and I'll pet him from time to time, so it won't arouse any suspicion. Then, heaven forbid, if it does look like I'm in danger, I'll give him whichever command seems appropriate. Thank you. I wouldn't attend the meeting without him."

"If it's any consolation, if I were in your shoes, I'm not so sure I'd be able to either."

At 2:15, Liz said, "I want to take Winston for a walk before we go to Walter's office. I'll be back in a few minutes, and then we can leave. I'm curious to see what Detective Latham has in mind."

CHAPTER THIRTY

Liz, Michelle, Roger, Sean, and Detective Latham were all seated in Walter's office when he began to speak. "We have about an hour and a half to go over the plans for the meeting in Dr. Throckmorton's office. Mitch, why don't you tell us what you have in mind?"

Detective Latham said, "First of all, I want to tell you that the detective I spoke of yesterday evening confirmed everything that Sean had found out. Dr. Throckmorton has been on his department's radar for a long time, but they just haven't been able to get the necessary evidence needed to bring charges against him." He turned to Sean, "He said he didn't know how you found out as much as you did and as quickly as you did, but if you ever need a job, he wants you to call his department." Everyone laughed.

"Thanks," Sean said. "I did a lot more research today and while only one new thing came to light, which I'll tell you about in a minute, what I did find out is that my initial information is absolutely correct. The doctor's seriously in debt, his wife is running up more and more debts every day, and there have been a number of complaints filed against him, but nothing that would stand up in a court of law. I'm glad that your friend was able to concur with my findings."

"Sean, you said you had something new. What's that?" Roger asked.

"I found out that Dr. Throckmorton has been seeing a psychiatrist twice a week. Evidently he's on several medications for severe depression and has talked to the doctor about committing suicide if his wife leaves him. He's terrified that if he has to curb her spending habits, that's what will happen."

"Sean, that's information between a doctor and a patient and as I recall, it's privileged and confidential. How were you able to find out something like that?" Detective Latham asked.

"Detective, law enforcement personnel often have their hands tied when it comes to getting information. As a private investigator, I don't. And as far as telling you how I found out or who told me, let me remind you of an applicable saying. If I tell you, I'll have to kill you."

Detective Latham laughed. "Okay, I get your point, but it doesn't thrill me. Not only are we dealing with someone who operates in a very grey area of medical practice, and may be a murderer, now we find out he could be suicidal. Swell. Michelle, how are you holding up?"

"I'm doing very well, Detective. Winston's been with me ever since our meeting last night, and even given what you just said, I'm not concerned." Michelle bent down and patted Winston. "I know he'll be with me when I'm in the meeting with Dr. Throckmorton, and if I feel threatened in any way, Liz has shown me two touch commands which will disable the doctor." She smiled and said, "I just hope something comes of this, and I will no longer be considered a suspect."

"If it makes you feel better, Michelle, although you were on my list simply because of your relationship with Bernie, I never really considered you to be a serious suspect," Detective Latham said, smiling broadly at her.

"Detective, you'll never know how much better that makes me feel."

"All right, now that we've gone over those things, I want to spend some time on the actual meeting. First of all, Liz, I believe you're going to take Michelle to the doctor's office and wait in the reception area while she's in the meeting with him. Is that correct?"

Liz nodded. "Yes, unless there's something else you'd like me to do."

"No. That's fine. We spoke yesterday about Michelle telling the doctor she's been seeing a psychiatrist, and that's the reason Winston is with her, as her comfort dog. I want you to do that, Michelle. If for any reason the doctor refuses to allow Winston in his office, I don't want you to go in by yourself. You'll have to tell him that Winston goes with you or you won't go in. Understand?"

"Yes, and I couldn't agree more. Although I'm not seeing a psychiatrist, Winston really has become a comfort to me."

"Michelle here's the next thing," the detective said as he took a small case out of his pocket. He opened it and took a ring from it. "This is a recording device. It looks like a big emerald, but of course it's fake. I really doubt that the doctor could tell the difference, it's so well done, but even if he does know something about jewelry, he'd have to examine it with a jeweler's loupe and a strong light, and I don't see that happening, given his obsession with the $500,000.

"I want you to wear it on your left hand, ring finger. He may want to shake hands with you and the tiny switch to activate it is just off to the side. That's why I don't want you to wear it on your right hand. I don't think it would be noticeable to him, but I don't want to take any chances." He handed the ring to her. "I want you to activate it the minute he comes into the reception area to get you."

"How do you know he won't send one of his nurses to get me?" Michelle asked.

"I checked his office schedule, and he closes at 3:00 on Thursdays. Today is Thursday, so the staff will all be gone, which is probably why he wanted to see you then. No one will be in the office or the reception area."

"All right. I can do that."

Detective Latham turned towards Roger and Walter. "I want both of you to follow Michelle and Liz to his office. Give them a two minute or so lead and then stand outside the doctor's office in the hallway. I have listening devices for both of you as well as Michelle's bodyguard. Roger, I'd like you to see to it that her bodyguard gets one.

"You can secure them behind your ears. They have a very fine clear thread and a listening device that will fit into your ear. That way you'll know when Michelle has gone into his office. You'll be able to hear everything that's being said between the two of them." He reached into his briefcase, took out three plastic cases, and handed one to Walter and two to Roger.

"Should I see if it works now?" Walter asked.

"No. When I finish telling you the plans, we'll spend some time making sure the devices are in good working order and that you know how to operate them. My staff and I tested everything shortly before I left my office, and all of the devices worked. Now to where my men and I will be."

"You're going to be there, too? Isn't it going to be a little crowded?" asked Liz.

"I had two of my men go over to the office building this morning to see what they could find out. After Michelle and the doctor go into his office for the meeting, three police officers and I will enter the reception area and stand in the hallway outside the doctor's office. In the event there's a problem, we will be in his office in a matter of seconds. If there isn't a problem, as soon as it's apparent the meeting is ending we'll move back to the outside hallway before he opens the door. So, Walter and Roger, do you feel that given what I've just told you, your client's safety will be assured?"

Roger looked over at Walter. "I'm okay with it, Walter. What about you?"

Walter looked over at Michelle and said, "Michelle, what Roger and I think isn't half as important as what you think. Do these plans sound okay to you?"

She nodded and said softly, "Yes. I'll just be glad when this is over, and I can start spending all my time getting ready for the twins."

"All right, if no one else has anything to add, I want to spend the remainder of the time here making sure everyone is comfortable with their equipment," Detective Latham said.

At 4:40 he said, "I just thought of one other thing I meant to tell you. Michelle, if the doctor shows you the document he says you signed, ask if he'll give you a copy of it. I'd like to have it examined if you can get it, but if he's forged your signature, I doubt that he'll give you a copy. And I did check to make sure he has a copier in his office. On the chance he'd give you a copy of it, I don't want him walking out into the hall where we are to make a copy. Okay, everything's working. Let's go. My men are on their way now. See you in a little while."

"Wait a minute," Sean said. "I told you I have to coach a soccer game this evening, but would someone do me a favor and text me or send me an email and let me know what's happened? I may be involved in coaching a game, but I'm also going to be thinking of what's happening with all of you. Good luck."

CHAPTER THIRTY-ONE

Liz opened the door to the doctor's reception area, and Michelle and Winston followed her in. They took a seat and Winston positioned himself between them. They'd only been sitting there a few moments when a handsome man wearing a doctor's lab coat opened the door to the reception room.

"Hello, Dr. Throckmorton," Michelle said. "I'd like you to meet my friend, Liz. She drove me here, and this is my dog, Winston."

Liz and the doctor shook hands and he said, "My staff makes sure that there's always the latest magazines here, so help yourself to them. Michelle, please come with me."

Michelle said, "Winston, come," as she stood up and began to follow the doctor.

"What are you doing?" he asked in confusion. "Why is that dog coming with you?"

"I've been so distraught over everything that's happened, I've started seeing a psychiatrist, and she recommended that I get a comfort dog. I feel much more stress free and comfortable when Winston's with me. He's well-trained, and he won't be a bother, I promise."

The doctor looked skeptically at Winston and said, "I'm not a big fan of dogs, but I guess it's okay." The two of them, along with Winston, entered his office and as he closed the door behind him, he said, "Please, have a seat and make yourself comfortable."

"Doctor, you mentioned that I'd signed something that indicated that when I delivered the twins and they received their inheritance, I'd owe you $500,000. I don't remember signing something like that. I'd like to see it," she said.

"I'm sorry, my dear, but that's impossible," he said smoothly. "I keep records like that in a safe deposit box at my bank, but let me assure you that you did in fact sign such a document."

"Dr. Throckmorton, you can't possibly expect me to pay you that kind of money without some documentation. Could you get it the next time you go to the bank? I might have signed a consent form for the procedure, but I barely remember that."

"Ahh, Michelle. That's true. You signed two forms, one was a consent form, and the other was the contract to pay me after the babies are born. I also keep all of my consent forms in the safe deposit box, in case there's ever a problem over a procedure. My insurance carrier requires it."

"Doctor, I can't believe you expect me to pay you when you won't even show me what I signed. I'm under enough pressure with being considered a suspect in Bernie's death now that it's been determined he was murdered. Believe me, the last thing I need is any more stress."

Winston was very attuned to the agitated sound of her voice and pressed against her. Michelle reached down and began to pet him.

"You'll be cleared when the police realize you don't have access to Propofol. The person who killed Bernie was probably just someone he'd irritated over the years and was looking for revenge."

"How did you know Propofol caused his death?" Michelle asked, continuing to stroke Winston. She could feel his muscles start to tense.

"I must have read it in the paper," Dr. Throckmorton said. "Yes, I remember reading an article about how it was the same drug that killed Michael Jackson. I thought that was rather ironic."

Michelle's eyes narrowed. "Doctor, it was never in the paper. The police deliberately kept that fact from the public hoping that whoever did it would trip themselves up by referring to it, and you just did."

The doctor abruptly stood up from his desk and said angrily, "Are you accusing me of being involved in Bernie Spitzer's murder? I may have been involved, but let me tell you something. You breathe a word of it to anyone, and I'll tell the authorities that you came to me and asked for the drug. I'll say I didn't want to give it to you. That's when you told me you'd give me $500,000 if I would give you the drug and then you could get pregnant. That's what I'll say, and it will be a liar's contest. Your word against mine. The word of a bimbo like you against a prominent doctor like me.

"I think we both know who people will believe. You breathe one word of this, and I'll make sure you spend the rest of your life in prison, and your babies, if you're lucky enough to have them, in some stinking foster home and you know what's that like." The whole time he'd been speaking his voice had gotten louder and louder, and he was gesturing wildly with his hands and arms. His eyes were nearly bulging out of their sockets and a drop of spittle was starting to run out of the corner of his mouth. He had clearly lost control of himself.

Michelle reached down and pressed her knuckle under Winston's jaw, and in one lightning fast movement the big powerful dog had the doctor pinned flat on the floor. He stood over him growling and snarling, his open mouth only inches from Dr. Throckmorton's face. At that moment, the door burst open and the four police officers ran into the room, guns drawn.

A moment later, Walter and Roger ran into the room, followed by Liz. Walter sat down beside Michelle and pulled her to him, whispering softly, "It's okay, everything's okay. The nightmare is over."

Detective Latham turned to Roger and said, "Give the command to Winston to release the doctor."

"Winston, stand down," Roger said in a firm voice. Winston walked over to where Michelle was sitting and calmly sat down next to her.

"I'm sick," the doctor said. "I'm going to throw up. I have to get to my bathroom." He lurched over to the door in the corner of the room and walked into it, while two of the policemen stood outside next to the door.

Seconds later the sound of a gunshot came from the bathroom. One of the policemen threw the door open and saw the doctor slumped over the toilet seat, a bullet hole in the side of his head. The policemen reached down to see if he could detect a pulse. There was none. The toilet tank cover was upended, exposing duct tape on the underneath side which had been used to secure the gun from view, the gun that ultimately ended his life.

Once it was determined that Dr. Throckmorton was dead, Detective Latham walked over to where Michelle and Walter were sitting and said, "Why don't you take her home? She's had enough stress, and I don't want to be the one to put any more on her. I'll need statements from both of you, but that can wait until tomorrow." He faced Michelle directly and said, "I thank you, my department thanks you, and the city thanks you. I know this didn't end the way any of us had anticipated, but without your help he'd be free to extort money, and who knows what else, from other women. You're the one who really unlocked this case. Now, go home and rest. You earned it."

EPILOGUE

DETECTIVE LATHAM: He thinks a lot about the Spitzer case and has even been a guest for dinner at Michelle and Walter's home. They've formed a bond based on murder. Not a bond everyone would expect, but Mitch felt he'd lived with the case for so long, it had become a part of who he was.

When he was able to get the necessary papers from the court to open Dr. Throckmorton's safe deposit box, he found the paper Michelle had supposedly signed. His handwriting expert told him it was a forgery and would have been thrown out of court if it had come to that. It didn't.

Although the autopsy indicated Bernie had died from a Propofol overdose injection, he couldn't figure out how the doctor had gained access to Bernie's condominium and why Bernie had allowed the doctor to give him an injection. It was explained by the tapes of recorded telephone conversations the doctor had in his safe deposit box. It turned out the doctor routinely recorded confidential telephone conversations with his patients that were of a highly sensitive nature. It appeared he used those recorded conversations to augment his income by blackmailing those patients in exchange for not divulging their confidences.

But what really got the detective's attention was a recorded telephone conversation between Bernie and the doctor on the night

Bernie died. Bernie had called Dr. Throckmorton's office to cancel his second appointment for the testosterone injections the doctor had prescribed for him in response to Bernie's complaint that he felt tired and lethargic most of the time. Bernie told him something had come up, and he would have to reschedule his appointment. The doctor said he was going to be attending a dinner near where Bernie lived, so he would be happy to stop by on his way to the dinner and give Bernie the injection.

Bernie said that solved his problem and he'd call the doorman and instruct him to let the doctor in and use his key for the elevator. He told him he was just getting ready to go to a charity event, so he asked him to hurry. It cleared up the mystery for the detective of how a murder victim dressed in a tuxedo could die from an overdose injection of Propofol, while he was living alone in a high security condominium. As they say, the rest was history.

MICHELLE: She gave birth to Chloe and Liam Spitzer and was appointed by the court as the guardian of their financial estates until they attained the age of eighteen. She's kept busy taking care of the twins and overseeing the one-quarter interest each of them received from Bernie's estate. She and Walter were married immediately after the children were born in a small private ceremony in her condominium with Liz and Roger serving as the witnesses. Michelle felt she owed it to Bernie to delay the wedding until his children were born.

She also became the owner of a beautiful adult female white boxer, Pearl, who she bought from Ed James. The dog had been raised in the James home, and was wonderful with the children. She says she's never been happier, and judging by the continuous smile on Walter's face, marriage and step-parenting two babies definitely agrees with him.

SEAN: He continues to do a spectacular job finding out things for the firm's lawyers that no one else is able to, but he never divulges his sources. Sean loves what he does, but insists that the best moment of his life was when the youth soccer team he coaches won the league championship. Liz decided he needs a wife, and has made finding a suitable woman for him a priority. She's asked him to come to the spa as her guest and plans on introducing him to Gina. Who knows?

ROGER: The satellite law office he runs for his firm in Red Cedar has become extremely successful. He still has to go into San Francisco occasionally for partnership meetings at the firm, and he's actively looking for an associate to help with the workload at the Red Cedar office. To Liz's chagrin, he's still one of Gertie's most loyal lunch customers.

LIZ: The spa has never been busier and she and her manager, Bertha, are thinking about expanding it. She's back to cooking the dinners for the spa guests who are staying in the cottages and even though Gina was very gracious to say she enjoyed doing it by herself, she definitely was glad to have Liz back.

WINSTON: He's in his usual place, which is wherever Liz is, since his main thing in life is making sure she's all right. Occasionally he thinks about the steak and hamburger he got when he stayed with Michelle, but Liz has loosened up a little and occasionally gives him leftover treats from the dinners she prepares for the guests. All in all, it's a pretty good life. Of course, a little filet mignon would make it even better.

RECIPES

ULLA'S SPLIT PEA SOUP

Ingredients:
3 cups dried green split peas
8 cups water
2 cups chicken broth (Canned or made from a concentrate is fine. Homemade is best, but who has that kind of time?)
1 Vidalia or other kind of sweet onion, chopped fine
3 Italian sausages, cooked in microwave or browned on stove top (Your call whether to use hot or regular), cut into ½ inch round pieces
1 tsp. salt
½ tsp. white pepper (If I'm out of it, I use black pepper.)
½ tsp. dried thyme

Directions:
Pour the water into a large pot. Add the peas and chicken stock and bring to a boil for two minutes. Remove from heat and let stand for one hour. Add the onion, sausage, salt, pepper, and thyme. Return pot to burner, cover and turn heat to medium-low. Cook until the peas become soft, approximately 45 minutes. Taste to see if more salt is needed. Ladle into bowls and enjoy!

CHICKEN CAESAR SALAD WITH DRESSING

Ingredients:
2 heads romaine lettuce (A lot of grocery stores carry prewashed and cut up romaine lettuce for Caesar salads. If you're short on time, might want to pick one up instead of preparing the lettuce.)
½ cup grated Parmesan cheese (Grate your own or use the pre-grated in the refrigerator section.)
4 skinless chicken breasts
1 cup Italian dressing (I used bottled. It's easier.)
1 cup croutons

Dressing Ingredients:
2 tbsp. red wine vinegar
1 ½ tsp. Worcestershire sauce
1 tsp. fresh lemon juice
1 tsp. dry ground mustard
½ cup extra virgin olive oil
Salt and pepper to taste.

Directions:
Cut each chicken breast in half lengthwise, then lightly pound chicken breasts until about ½ inch thick. Cut breasts into pieces that are approximately 2" x 4". Marinate the chicken pieces in the Italian dressing for 3 hours.

Chop or shred the romaine lettuce. If you're not going to serve it immediately, you can store it in the refrigerator in a plastic bag.

Dressing preparation. Combine all of the ingredients in a food processor with the exception of the olive oil. Pulse to blend. Add olive oil in a slow stream until the mixture is emulsified. Add salt and pepper. (This can be made ahead of time and refrigerated.)

Grill the marinated chicken on a hot BBQ grill for approximate 3 to 4 minutes on each side.

Mix the romaine lettuce, croutons, and ¼ cup of Parmesan cheese in a large bowl. Add the dressing and toss the salad. (You may wish to use a portion of the dressing, rather than all of it. Your choice.) Divide the romaine mixture among four plates. Top with the chicken pieces and the remaining Parmesan cheese. Serve and enjoy!

DARK AND LIGHT CHOCOLATE CHEESECAKE

Ingredients:

Crust:
2 ½ cups graham cracker crumbs
7 tbsp. butter, melted
1/8 tsp. salt
Cheesecake:
40 oz. cream cheese
5 eggs (I like jumbo.)
2 egg yolks
2 tsp. vanilla
1 ¾ cups sugar
1/8 cup all-purpose flour
¼ cup heavy cream
4 oz. dark chocolate
6 oz. white chocolate
10-inch springform pan

Directions:
Bring eggs, cream cheese, and cream to room temperature. Preheat oven to 350 degrees.

Combine graham cracker crumbs, sugar, salt, and melted butter in a large bowl. Once combined, press into bottom of 10-inch springform pan and 1 inch up the sides. Bake in preheated oven for 10 minutes. Remove from oven and cool completely on a rack.

Using an electric mixer, combine the cream cheese, eggs, egg yolks, and vanilla in a bowl. Add in the sugar, flour, and heavy cream until thoroughly incorporated. (You may have some small lumps.)

Melt the two chocolates separately in a microwave or in saucepans on the stove top. When melted, let cool for 5 minutes.

Stir 1/3 of the egg batter into the pan with the melted dark chocolate. Stir the melted white chocolate into the bowl containing the remaining egg batter.

Pour 1/3 of the white chocolate batter onto the crust. Drop one large spoonful of the dark chocolate batter at a time on top. Pour the remaining white chocolate batter over it. Using a knife, gently swirl the mixture.

Turn the oven up to 400 degrees and bake for 15 minutes. Reduce heat to 200 degrees and bake for 3 hours. Turn oven off and slightly open the oven door. Let cheesecake remain in oven for 1 hour. Remove from oven, cool completely, cover with plastic wrap, and chill in refrigerator for 24 hours.

When ready to serve remove springform pan sides. Serve and enjoy!

NOTE: I've made a lot of different cheesecake recipes over the years and this is absolutely the best!

TOM'S SHRIMP ALFREDO

Ingredients:
1 lb. linguine pasta
2 tbsp. unsalted butter
1 ½ lbs. raw shrimp, peeled and deveined with tails removed

Alfredo Sauce:
½ cup unsalted butter
½ cup heavy cream
½ cup Parmesan cheese, grated (Do it yourself or get the pre-grated in the refrigerator section of your supermarket.)
2 cloves garlic, minced

Salt and pepper to taste

Directions:
Bring a large pot of water to a boil. Add 2 tablespoons of salt. Add the linguine and cook according to package directions. Turn off heat, drain and return to pot.

Melt butter in a medium saucepan over medium heat. Add garlic and cook for 1 minute. Add cream and Parmesan cheese to saucepan and reduce heat to low, whisking occasionally.

While the sauce is simmering, start the shrimp. In a large skillet, melt 2 tbsp. butter over medium heat. Add shrimp and cook for 3 minutes per side until pink. Don't overcook!

Add shrimp to the pasta and pour the sauce over it. Toss to combine and coat the pasta.

Plate and enjoy!

BAKED APPLES

Ingredients:
4 large baking apples
4 tbsp. butter, softened
½ cup brown sugar
¾ tsp. cinnamon
¼ cup chopped pecans

Directions:
Preheat oven to 375 degrees. Wash and core the apples, but leave enough of the apple to contain the filling.

Combine butter, brown sugar, cinnamon, and chopped pecans. Separate the mixture into four parts and fill each apple with one part.

Fill a baking dish with about ¾ cup water. Place the apples

upright in the dish. Bake in oven for approximately 1 hour or until the apples are soft and the filling is browned. Cut in pieces, serve, and enjoy!

NOTE: We have two apple trees, so I'm always looking for ways to serve apples in the fall. This is great with pork.

Paperbacks & Ebooks for FREE

Go to www.dianneharman.com/freepaperback.html and get your FREE copies of Dianne's books and favorite recipes immediately by signing up for her newsletter.

Once you've signed up for her newsletter you're eligible to win three paperbacks. One lucky winner is picked every week. Hurry before the offer ends!

ABOUT THE AUTHOR

Dianne lives in Huntington Beach, California, with her husband, Tom, a former California State Senator, and her boxer dog, Kelly. Her passions are cooking, reading, and dogs, so whenever she has a little free time, you can either find her in the kitchen, playing with Kelly in the back yard, or curled up with the latest book she's reading.

Her award winning books include:

Cedar Bay Cozy Mystery Series
Kelly's Koffee Shop, Murder at Jade Cove, White Cloud Retreat, Marriage and Murder, Murder in the Pearl District, Murder in Calico Gold, Murder at the Cooking School, Murder in Cuba, Trouble at the Kennel, Murder on the East Coast, Trouble at the Animal Shelter, Murder & The Movie Star, Murdered by Wine

Cedar Bay Cozy Mystery Series - Boxed Set
Cedar Bay Cozy Mysteries 1 (Books 1 to 3)
Cedar Bay Cozy Mysteries 2 (Books 4 to 6)
Cedar Bay Cozy Mysteries 3 (Books 7 to 10)
Cedar Bay Cozy Mysteries 4 (Books 11 to 13)
Cedar Bay Super Series (Books 1 to 6)... good deal
Cedar Bay Uber Series (Books 1 to 9)... great deal

Liz Lucas Cozy Mystery Series
Murder in Cottage #6, Murder & Brandy Boy, The Death Card, Murder at The Bed & Breakfast, The Blue Butterfly, Murder at the Big T Lodge, Murder in Calistoga, Murder in San Francisco

Liz Lucas Cozy Mystery Series - Boxed Set
Liz Lucas Cozy Mysteries 1 (Books 1 to 3)
Liz Lucas Cozy Mysteries 2 (Books 4 to 6)
Liz Lucas Super Series (Books 1 to 6)... good deal

High Desert Cozy Mystery Series
Murder & The Monkey Band, Murder & The Secret Cave, Murdered by Country Music, Murder at the Polo Club, Murdered by Plastic Surgery

High Desert Cozy Mystery Series - Boxed Set
High Desert Cozy Mysteries 1 (Books 1 to 3)

Northwest Cozy Mystery Series
Murder on Bainbridge Island, Murder in Whistler, Murder in Seattle, Murder after Midnight

Northwest Cozy Mystery Series - Boxed Set
Northwest Cozy Mysteries 1 (Books 1 to 3)

Midwest Cozy Mystery Series
Murdered by Words, Murder at the Clinic

Jack Trout Cozy Mystery Series
Murdered in Argentina

Coyote Series
Blue Coyote Motel, Coyote in Provence, Cornered Coyote

Midlife Journey Series
Alexis

Newsletter

If you would like to be notified of her latest releases please go to www.dianneharman.com and sign up for her newsletter.

Website: www.dianneharman.com,
Blog: www.dianneharman.com/blog
Email: dianne@dianneharman.com

NEW BOOK BY KATHI DALEY - The Christmas Letter

You may be familiar with my friend Kathi Daley's cozy mystery books, but if not, you're in for a treat. Here's some information about her latest one (available on Amazon). Enjoy!

And a bit about The Christmas Letter:

If you love small towns, endearing relationships, food, animals, and a touch of murder, you will love this new mystery series by Kathi Daley, author of the popular Zoe Donovan Cozy Mystery Series. Set in the small town of White Eagle Montana, the series features Tess and her dog Tilly, who spend their days delivering the latest gossip along with the daily mail. When a member of the community is murdered, Tess and Tilly join forces with a mysterious friend, to sleuth out the truth behind the shocking murder that is rocking the tight knit community.

Here's the link to the book on Amazon:
https://www.amazon.com/Christmas-Letter-Cozy-Mystery-Tilly-ebook/dp/B075RR9JX3

or go straight to Amazon by scanning the QR code below using your smartphone. Open your QR code app (available for FREE online), point the phone at this code and you're done.

Made in the USA
Columbia, SC
04 July 2019